AF172788

The Eagle's Nest

by

S. E. Cartwright

Double 9
BOOKS

The Eagle's Nest
by S. E. Cartwright

Copyright © 2023

All Rights reserved.

No part of this publication may be reproduced, stored in a retrieval system, or transmitted in any form or by any means, electronic, mechanical, photocopying or Otherwise, without the written permission of the publisher.
The author/editor asserts the moral right to be identified as the author/editor of this work.

ISBN: 978-93-60461-35-5

Published by

DOUBLE 9 BOOKS

2/13-B, Ansari Road
Daryaganj, New Delhi – 110002
info@double9books.com
www.double9books.com
Tel. 011-40042856

This book is under public domain

ABOUT THE AUTHOR

S. E. Cartwright, a tremendous 19th-century creator, is widely known for his literary contribution, particularly his famend paintings, "The Eagle's Nest." This brightly written story unfolds around 3 nation-state kids who ingeniously construct a fascinating sanctuary in a beach tree on their father's farm. The narrative takes an exciting turn as the youngsters stumble upon Lewis Brand, unbeknownst to their dad and mom, adding layers of thriller and exhilaration to the story. "The Eagle's Nest" is hailed as one in every of S. E. Cartwright's masterpieces, showcasing his storytelling prowess and ability to captivate readers. The novel no longer handiest explores the innovative endeavors of the kids but also introduces a detail of suspense through the creation of Lewis Brand. Cartwright's writing fashion is characterised via a perfect combination of beauty and simplicity, making his tales available and exciting for readers of every age. His first rate narratives, including "The Eagle's Nest," stand as testaments to his talent in crafting engaging and noteworthy testimonies. With an artful combination of literary finesse and clarity, S. E. Cartwright invitations each person to immerse themselves in the enchanting worlds he creates, ensuring that his testimonies stay loved throughout generations.

CONTENTS

CHAPTER I
A WASP IN THE SCHOOLROOM

One bright May morning, Madge, Betty, and John were a little more inattentive than usual over their lessons. Miss Thompson was very patient. She knew that warm spring days were full of distracting interests. The first wasp of the season managed to get into the schoolroom and buzz ostentatiously on the window-pane in the middle of a history lesson. There was a long pause of expectation on the part of the three children. Surely even a grown-up person could not be so utterly uninterested as to allow a queen-wasp to escape alive?

"What was the chief event of the reign of Henry the Eighth?" continued Miss Thompson, quite unmoved by the display of suppressed excitement around her. There was no answer, so she repeated the question a little louder.

"May I kill it, or would you rather do it yourself?" said Madge eagerly. The three children had now shut their books and given up all pretence of interest in anything except the wasp, which was trying harder than ever to buzz right through the pane of glass.

"Really nobody would suppose that you were twelve years old!" said Miss Thompson, in a vain effort to make her eldest pupil ashamed of herself. "Now then, open your history and see what was the most important event, if you can't remember."

"But it'll get away if you don't squash it!" shrieked John and Betty. They were twins, and perhaps for that reason always spoke together.

"Do leave the poor creature alone!" said Miss Thompson imploringly. "It cannot hurt you if you sit still and attend to your lessons."

"That's not what we are afraid of!" cried Madge; "it's the fruit! Don't you know a queen-wasp has millions of children before the summer is over, and we shan't have any fruit at all if you don't kill it!"

"No strawberries! No peaches! No nothing!" echoed the twins with growing excitement. "And it will be all your fault! But of course you don't care, as you never eat fruit. Papa won't like it though. He always kills—"

"My dears, please don't make such a silly fuss about nothing," interrupted Miss Thompson, rising with considerable dignity from her seat. The children watched her with the most intense interest; but when, instead of crushing the intruding wasp, she merely tried to brush it out of the open window with her handkerchief, they broke out into shouts of disapproval. If the poor lady had let loose some peculiarly savage wild beast on society she could not have been more severely condemned by public opinion. And the worst of it was, that the wasp would not go! She clung to the handkerchief, and when it was shaken at the open window suddenly transferred herself to the sleeve of her deliverer's dress.

Even Miss Thompson's calmness gave way under this trial. She started back with a slight scream. The children were at her side in a moment, beating and slapping at her arm, until they had inflicted almost as much injury as a sting.

"It's fallen on the floor!" shrieked Madge. "No! it's up again! It's back on the window! Where's the squasher?"

There was one well-established way of killing wasps in the schoolroom at Beechgrove. This was with the heavy brass top of an old-fashioned ink-bottle. Its size and shape were all that could be desired, and it was familiarly alluded to as "the squasher". Even Miss Thompson when in a hurry sometimes forgot to describe it as the top of an ink-bottle, though she usually corrected herself afterwards.

At the present moment both Betty and John rushed to the table, and began to fight vigorously for the possession of the much-coveted instrument of destruction.

"Bring it quickly!" screamed Madge, who did not dare leave the window for fear of losing sight of her prey. "Bring it here, I say! You aren't going to squash it, you little sillies! I'm the eldest, so it's my place!"

"You unfair thing! You squashed the last, so it's my turn!" shouted John. And while he turned to hurl defiance at his elder sister, Betty seized the opportunity to twitch the object of strife out of his hand and run off with it.

Something perilously like a free-fight was in progress, when Miss Thompson recovered her self-possession and sternly ordered the children to return to their seats.

"And the wasp?" they cried. "It will get away, and make nests, and we shall be stung, and have no fruit, and—"

"I will kill it myself," interrupted Miss Thompson, who now saw that this was the only way to restore quiet.

"But why should you?" pleaded Madge. "You don't like squashing wasps, and we do."

"That's just the reason I am going to do it myself," said Miss Thompson resolutely. "Now go back to the table and find out the place in your books."

"You are very unkind. Yes, very unkind," grumbled the twins; but they did not dare to flatly disobey, any more than Madge, who left the window scowling horribly, and expressing an audible hope that everybody who liked wasps should be stung by wasps.

It was particularly annoying that Miss Thompson took no notice of this amiable speech, but after crushing the wasp with as little interest as she would have buttoned a glove, returned quietly to her seat, and inquired:

"What was the most important event in the reign of Henry the Eighth?" precisely as if nothing had happened.

"Oh, I know the answer to that!" exclaimed John scornfully. "I've known that since I was a baby!"

"Well then, why do you require me to repeat the question so many times?" very naturally observed Miss Thompson. "Do give me a sensible answer, and then I can pass on to something that you do not know so well."

"Oh, of course, it was about all his wives having their heads cut off—"

"Not all!" interrupted Betty. "Just let me say them! Catherine of Arragon was divorced, Anne Boleyn had—"

"Stop!" cried Miss Thompson. "You are both wrong."

"No! Really I am sure it's right!" exclaimed Betty. "Isn't it, Madge? You know you saw the place where her head was chopped off that time you went to London with Aunt Mabel. Nobody was allowed to walk on it, and there were railings all round; and the policeman said one night in the year her ghost—"

"Really this has nothing at all to do with your lesson," said Miss Thompson, resolutely cutting short what threatened to be a very long story. "I never doubted that Anne Boleyn was beheaded," she continued. "Only, as it happens, my question has nothing to do with Henry the Eighth's wives. Other events of much greater importance happened during his reign, though you seem to have forgotten them. The Reformation, for instance."

"Oh, you meant that sort of thing, did you?" said John, every spark of interest dying out of his voice. It might be possible to remember a few facts about axes and blocks, but church councils and acts of parliament he felt to be altogether beneath his notice. So he simply gave up even the pretence of attending, and began to stare out of the window at the gardener mowing the lawn. "Once, twice, three times," he counted, in a loud whisper, as the man passed the window with the mowing-machine.

"Draw down the blind, John," said Miss Thompson.

There was a chorus of reproaches from all the children. They particularly disliked this punishment, which was only inflicted on rare occasions when they had been unusually inattentive.

"Draw down the blind at once," repeated Miss Thompson.

"I always feel so gloomy when the blind is down," lamented Madge in a very mournful tone. "I know I can't do my lessons if the sun is all shut out."

"My dear, they couldn't have been done worse this morning if you had been shut up in the dark," replied Miss Thompson, trying to close the discussion by again taking up the history-book.

But by this time John had wandered to the window, and was carefully inspecting the dead wasp. Not content with looking, he must needs take it up to count how many legs it had. "One, two, three, four." John was very fond of counting, especially at lesson-times. But there was one important item that he left out of his calculations—the sting!

"Oh! oh! It hurts! it hurts!" shouted the little boy, as he hopped about the room nursing his thumb.

"You silly child! If you had only been obedient and done what I told you, instead of playing with the wasp," began Miss Thompson. Then she remembered that it really was a waste of breath pointing out a moral to a boy who was shouting and sobbing, so that he could not hear a word she said. "You had better go to the nursery," she added, "and have something put on your hand. No, you need not do any more lessons before dinner. You can go out into the garden, and your sisters will join you when they have finished."

John was out of the schoolroom door almost before she had done speaking. When once in the passage his cries stopped suddenly. He knew better than to wake the baby out of its mid-day sleep. So on tiptoe, with carefully suppressed sobs, he entered the nursery, and replied in whispers to Nurse's anxious inquiries after his injuries. John had been her favourite charge until the recent arrival of a baby brother. Now she was fickle enough to prefer the baby, or at least to behave as if she did. Still, she lavished much compassion in dumb-show on John's swollen thumb, and wrapped it in a blue bag, until he became so interested in the process that he quite forgot it was hurting. But presently Baby stirred in his sleep, and Nurse being anxious to attend to him, advised John to run out and play in the garden.

It was not strictly speaking kind, but at the same time it was very natural conduct, that John should stand close outside the schoolroom window making derisive faces at his two sisters, who were being reluctantly introduced to the leading facts of English history. Betty first noticed him, and broke into a loud giggle. Miss Thompson looked up.

"If you are well enough to stand there grimacing in the sun, you are well enough to come in and finish your lessons," was all she said. John promptly fled out of sight round the corner.

CHAPTER II
UNDER THE LABURNUM-TREE

Within a few yards of the schoolroom window, but just out of sight, stood a large laburnum-tree. Behind it was a very substantial bay-bush. The two were planted at a corner of the house, with the intention probably of cutting off a view of the kitchen windows from the front. But the children had elevated them into a far higher position than that of a mere screen. The laburnum-tree represented their parliament-house. In it, or under it, as the case might be, they played most of their games, told most of their stories, originated most of their schemes.

It was to this refuge that John fled when threatened with lessons. It was so conveniently near the schoolroom, that he could easily hear through the open window when lessons were over; for since he had gone out Miss Thompson had not punished the girls by making them sit behind a closed window and drawn blind. Besides, Madge and Betty were sure to join him under the laburnum-tree directly they were released. In the meantime John enjoyed the unwonted luxury of a choice of seats.

There was only one drawback to the laburnum. It was really such a nice tree that one hardly likes to mention this one fault, but if the children could have suggested any sort of improvement, it would have been a little more sitting accommodation in the boughs. Try as they would they could never, all three, get up in it at once. And John was usually the one left out. This was the way it happened. Madge, being two years older than the twins, and much larger, naturally always seized the highest and most commodious place. Then Betty, lightly observing, "Ladies before gentlemen," would creep into a narrow little fork between two branches at her sister's feet. And all that remained for John was a yard of slippery polished stem, on which nothing but a fly could have sat.

John grumbled—it was one of the things he did best, according to his sisters. "Practice makes perfect," Betty used to say, alluding to this habit of his. She was fond of proverbs, and introduced them into her conversation with more aptness than consideration for the feelings of others. But really about this matter of seats it did seem a little hard on John to have always to crouch in the bay-bush, while his sisters looked down on him from their lofty thrones,—even Betty's boots on a level with his head. Of course, they daily pointed out to him that the crushed bay leaves gave out a delicious smell. This was quite true, but it in no way removed the original grievance. One may have too much even of bay leaves.

However, this morning for about half an hour John had undisturbed possession of the laburnum-tree. He began by trying Madge's seat, but his legs being several inches shorter than hers dangled most uncomfortably, instead of reaching the bough below. In order to steady himself he had to hold on with one hand, which was terribly humiliating. Madge, who could sit there in the most unconcerned manner, plaiting rushes or carving a stick, would be sure to laugh at him if she came out and noticed his difficulty. He hastily slipped down into Betty's seat.

Now it so happened that the twins were not at all alike in appearance. John was a fine handsome boy, Betty rather a thin, under-sized girl; consequently the fork between the laburnum branches into which she fitted exactly would not admit her brother at all. Except for the glory of the thing, it was far safer and more comfortable down among the bay leaves. John was so seldom out in the garden without his sisters that he had never before had a quiet opportunity for making this discovery. He was still thinking it over with puzzled astonishment, when there was a loud sound of slamming doors, and Betty ran out of the house, dangling her straw hat from her hand by a worn-out bit of elastic.

"Madge kept in?" inquired John anxiously.

"Oh no! It's her turn to put away the books and desks, that's all."

This was a relief, for though the twins were supposed to be romantically devoted to each other, they were both in reality rather dependent upon Madge, whose superior size, age, and experience made her the undisputed leader in all their games. John and Betty waited impatiently, listening to the series of bangs which accompanied their sister's rather abrupt restoration of order in the schoolroom. At last there were three crashes louder than all the former sounds.

"Hurrah! There go the desks!" shouted John. "That's the last thing always. She'll be here in a minute!"

In point of fact Madge joined them almost immediately. "I've thought of something," she said, directly she came within shouting distance.

There was some excitement at this announcement, for when Madge solemnly observed that she had thought of something, it always meant that an unusually interesting plan was about to be unfolded. They all climbed into their customary seats to await further developments. As Betty was nearest the laburnum-tree she scrambled up first, so that Madge had presently to crawl right over her, even planting a pair of very substantial and dusty boots in her younger sister's lap; but this was by no means a sufficiently uncommon event to call for any remonstrance. As for John, he squatted down among the bay leaves much more contentedly than usual. He had just found out that those lofty seats up among the golden-chains, as the children called the laburnum blossom, were not half as comfortable as they looked.

"This is what I have been thinking," began Madge, when she had settled herself, not kicking Betty's head more than twice in the process. "We want some hiding-place where no one can find us."

"Yes! yes!" shouted the twins.

"Some place in a tree," continued Madge.

The applause became louder than ever. Climbing trees was the favourite amusement of all the children, and no game found favour for long which did not include something of the kind.

"A tree like this, will it be?" inquired Betty.

"Of course not," replied Madge. She had her own idea, and could not help feeling rather irritated with the younger ones for not entering into it without any explanations. "This is hardly like a real tree," she continued; "more like a garden-seat, you know. If we fell out of it, I don't believe we should be hurt a bit."

This statement was felt by the assembled company to be quite true, though perhaps a little ungrateful, seeing how very much use they made of the laburnum.

"Now, I should like a tree which would be a real fortress," continued Madge. "A regular place of refuge—"

"What is a refuge?" interrupted John.

"Why, a place of safety, of course! Where one can hide from the enemy and—"

"What enemy?" again interrupted John.

"Oh, don't be so tiresome!" broke in Betty, who always understood things a little quicker than her brother—or if not, pretended she did. "Can't you fancy an enemy? Men in armour, or lions, or Nurse when she wants us to be put to bed."

John did not answer, being a little sulky. Of course he could imagine enemies just as well as his sisters; worse ones perhaps, with longer spears and sharper teeth! And he did not like being considered silly.

"What I think," continued Madge, who was accustomed to talk through interruptions, so that she hardly noticed them; "what I think is that we ought to make a kind of house up in a big tree, so high that no grown-up people can possibly climb to it, and if we tumbled out we should break our legs."

"I am afraid none of the garden trees will do," said Betty thoughtfully, as she pondered over the required qualifications.

"Did I say it was to be in the garden?" snapped out Madge. "It will be in the fields—the farthest part of the fields. And," she added, leaning forward and whispering mysteriously, "I know the tree."

"Oh, which is it? Where is it?" shouted the twins. John's sulks at once gave place to his curiosity.

"It's the beech-tree by the wall at the end of the Pig's Field," announced Madge. "I have examined it, and it will do exactly."

"You do have such good plans!" murmured Betty admiringly. Indeed, an elder sister who can work out a project of this sort in her head without saying a word to anyone, is a member of the family of whom one may feel justly proud.

"But I hope there's a place for me in this grand tree of yours," observed John, in the accent of complaint that was rather habitual to him. "Because, if I've got to sit on the ground as I do here, and the enemy comes, it won't be very nice for me; though of course you two will be all right, so you won't care!" and he crushed the bay leaves viciously under his feet until the air became quite aromatic.

"If you would only listen to me instead of grumbling you would hear my whole plan," observed Madge, very reasonably. "We shall not sit on branches as we have always done before, we will build a house by putting sticks for a floor. A sort of huge nest, with lots of room for us all. Of course, if we build it ourselves, we can make it just as large or as small as we like."

The audience was positively struck dumb by the magnificent ingenuity of this new idea. The clanging sound of a large bell at last broke the silence.

"Oh, dear! There is dinner in five minutes!" sighed Betty, wriggling out of her narrow seat. "And I upset the ink-bottle over my hands, so that they will take longer to wash than usual, and there will be no time to hear the rest of your plan now, because I promised to bring Miss Thompson in a bunch of golden-chains." And she began pulling down the lowest boughs of the laburnum by swinging upon them with all her weight.

"All right!" said Madge good-naturedly; "I'll help." Climbing down to the ground, she began to tear large sprays of golden blossom off the boughs lowered by Betty's weight. "There, I should think that's enough!" she said, when her two hands were full to overflowing. "Now we had better run in, or we shall be late and lose our punctuality marks! But first I will tell you both one more thing. I have even thought of a name for this house in the tree. The Eagle's Nest. What do you say to that?" But the twins' admiration and enthusiasm for their elder sister could not find a vent in mere words.

CHAPTER III
THE EAGLE'S NEST

A good name is half the battle. That the Eagle's Nest was going to be a magnificent success all the children felt at once. Fortunately it was Saturday, and there were no lessons to be done after dinner, so they had a whole long afternoon in which to lay the foundations of their new house.

When Captain West married and left the navy, many years before our story begins, he had bought Beechgrove and the little farm attached to the house. So his children had no lack of fields and outhouses in which to play, directly they were old enough for Nurse to trust them out of her sight. The only rule that they were bound to observe was: Never to go off their father's property. This was not often felt to be an oppressive regulation, for the dozen fields of which the farm consisted contained untold treasures, in the way of hedges rich in birds' nests, and green slimy ponds alive with newts and tadpoles. The fact was, that the children had never yet found any day long enough to explore the fields to their entire satisfaction.

But there was one corner of the Beechgrove farm which seemed more mysteriously interesting than all the rest. In the first place, it was at an immense distance from the house; a grown-up person on a hot day would very likely have taken nearly a quarter of an hour to walk there. The children, of course, took much longer; they never went straight anywhere, and even if they started to run they forgot half-way where they were going, and wandered off in several directions, after passing objects of interest, before they remembered. So, excepting on long summer afternoons, they very seldom got as far as this particular corner, where the beech-trees grew in such abundance as to give their name to the whole place.

There was another reason as well as its remoteness from civilization which made the children regard this corner with a peculiarly awe-struck interest. On the other side of the high wall which bounded the farm at this end lived an old lady, about whom most extraordinary stories were told. She was undoubtedly eccentric and fond of seclusion, as she had spent a large sum of money on fencing her little property entirely round with a stone wall about ten feet high. Also, she never went for walks; and it was said that tradesmen's carts were not admitted into the garden, but had to wait outside on the road while the old housekeeper carried all they brought through a door in the wall, which she carefully closed behind her. Nobody but the clergyman and the doctor had been admitted to see Mrs. Howard for years; and they were neither of them gossips, so the neighbourhood did not learn much after their visits. Some people said that the old lady was mad; others that she had committed some terrible crime for which she had been sentenced to imprisonment for life, but that being very rich, she had been allowed to escape this disgrace on condition of paying a huge fine and promising never to go outside those gloomy high walls.

The children firmly believed all the different stories they had been told by successive nursery-maids, and even a legend started by the old weeding-woman, to the effect that Mrs. Howard belonged to a very high family living in London, and that having gone mad she took advantage of her position to shoot at the Queen as she was driving through Hyde Park. The story broke off at this point, which was so unsatisfactory that the children teased Mrs. Bunn to try and remember more, until, being in a hurry to get on with her weeding, she hazarded a suggestion that perhaps the poor lady was so mad that she forgot to load the pistol. As the Queen continued to live and reign, this really seemed very probable.

Of course the little Wests could have asked their parents about Mrs. Howard, and found out from them something more nearly approaching the truth. But on the whole they very much preferred being at liberty to believe all sorts of wonderful and terrible reports. It is such hard work to satisfy one's natural craving for romantic adventure when one is carefully brought up in a well-guarded nursery and schoolroom, that it would be mere stupid ingratitude not to get all the excitement one could out of a mysterious neighbour.

After this explanation, it can be better understood how very bold and thrilling a proposal Madge made when she suggested that the Eagle's Nest should be built in a beech-tree that actually overhung the boundary wall.

"How are we to begin? What shall we do first?" inquired the twins, as with business-like rapidity the three children started off across the fields immediately after their dinner. For once none of them lingered to pick buttercups, or even hunt the pigs.

"First we make the floor," said Madge, who was in a very good humour at being so undoubtedly leader of the expedition. "Until that is made we have nothing to stand on while we are putting up the roof."

This was unquestionably true; besides, everybody felt that though a very fairly satisfactory nest could be imagined open to the sky, some sort of floor was an absolute necessity in a tree-house.

"But where shall we get the boards and nails from?" asked John, thinking of the neat planks he had so often counted in the nursery.

"Boards and nails!" laughed Madge. "Do you think it's going to be exactly like the stupid sort of houses we are used to? Perhaps you expect to see a brown carpet with red spots, like the one in the schoolroom?"

"Of course not! Don't be so silly!" cried John angrily. But all the same, it must be confessed he could not imagine a house very unlike Beechgrove.

"You see, this will be more of a nest," interposed Betty; "so it ought to be made of sticks."

"That's it! Follow me and I will show you where to get some." And Madge set off running across the field, closely pursued by the two others.

It was not very difficult to guess where the sticks were to be found. Every winter the wind had a delightful way of blowing down some large boughs on the farm, and these used to be cut up and stacked together until wanted for various purposes. The children regarded these windfalls as expressly designed for their convenience and amusement. They climbed on the heavier logs, which were piled into temptingly irregular mountains several feet high; and of the smaller sticks they made every kind of defensive weapon.

Madge led the way straight to one of these wood-piles. After much study she chose several small branches, and all three children, producing knives out of their pockets, set to work hacking off unnecessary twigs. The twigs being extremely tough and the knives not at all sharp, this process took a long time, and the afternoon seemed to be going by without their even coming in sight of Eagle's Nest.

"It's really no good trying to tidy up these sticks here!" Madge cried at last in despair. "Let us each carry as many branches as we can to the Eagle's Nest, and we can trim them into shape there when we see exactly what we want."

This seemed a particularly good idea, as all their hands were aching after sawing away for so long with their blunt knives at the hard wood. So a procession set out, each child dragging a branch along the ground. By doing it that way they could move good-sized branches which would afterwards cut up into several sticks.

"Oh, Madge, it's perfect! It's quite perfect!" cried the twins some time later, when, hot and panting, they at last dropped their burdens beneath the great beech-tree by the wall.

"I really think it's pretty good," replied Madge modestly. She felt that as she had invented this plan herself it would not be good manners for her to admire it too freely. "You see those two boughs poking out like great arms over the field? The sticks must be long enough to stretch from one to the other, and the Eagle's Nest when it is built will be between them."

"Oh, why did we never think of it before!" exclaimed Betty, rolling on the ground in an ecstasy of admiration.

"Well, you know we don't often come into this corner of the field to look about," Madge reminded her; "it's so far from the house. And besides," she added frankly, "I used to be rather afraid of coming here without Nurse when I was smaller, because of Mrs. Howard."

A shade of anxiety passed over the younger children's faces. They had forgotten all about that mysterious old lady behind the wall, with her terrible character for madness and crime. Yet she was possibly lurking within a few yards of them, even listening to what they were saying.

"Do you think," began John seriously, "are you sure, that it's quite safe here?"

"Quite safe," asserted Madge decidedly. "If Mrs. Howard tried to come an inch this side of the wall she would be a trespasser, and we could send a policeman after her."

An elder sister who has mastered the law of trespass to this extent is really an invaluable possession. John's mind was quite set at rest, and with a sigh of relief he again pulled out his knife and began hacking away at a branch.

"I dare say you are both wondering how we are going to get up to the Eagle's Nest," said Madge. "Now I will show you."

She went to the wall against which the beech-tree was growing, and deliberately put her toe into a deep crack between the stones where the mortar had fallen out. The others watched with the greatest excitement, while, partly supported by inequalities on the trunk of the tree, and partly taking advantage of projecting stones in the wall, she slowly climbed up until she was on a level with the destined foundations of the Eagle's Nest.

"Now hand me up a branch," she cried, "and I will lay the first stone of our house!"

"But I thought you said it was to be all sticks?" objected John.

"Do try and not be stupid!" exclaimed Betty rather sharply, as she wrestled with a branch far beyond her strength to lift single-handed. "One always talks of laying the first stone, you know, whatever the place is built of. At least I never heard of laying the first brick! And please help me to lift up the end of this branch, I can't push it high enough, and it will get entangled in my hair and knock off my hat."

The twins struggled unsuccessfully to lift the heavy branch high enough for Madge to reach. She stooped forward as far as she dared, almost losing her balance indeed, in her effort to get hold of this refractory foundation-stone. "If you two were only a little taller!" she exclaimed reproachfully.

Betty looked down abashed. She was short for her age, and knew it. Quite an inch more in the wrong than John. But she had ideas.

"If we knotted all our handkerchiefs together and tied them to one end of the branch, you could pull it up easily," she suggested.

In ten minutes more the first stick, or stone, of the Eagle's Nest was laid amidst shouts of congratulation and rejoicing.

CHAPTER IV
A ROPE-LADDER

Building even the most simple sort of house is a very great work. A nest ought to be begun and finished in less than a week—at least year after year birds accomplish something of the sort without our ever thinking them particularly clever or industrious. But the Eagle's Nest at Beechgrove was terribly incomplete, even after a fortnight's labour had been expended on it.

"It doesn't look as if it would ever be finished," said John mournfully, "and yet we have worked so hard."

His spirits were apt to give way when anything went wrong either at lessons or play, and the first sign of depression was that he sat still and did nothing.

"You see, making the steps up the wall took a very long time," said Betty, who was vigorously sawing away at some twigs with a knife that had lately lost the little edge it ever boasted. "But they are very good steps," she added proudly.

By scratching patiently with sharp stones and long-suffering knives, the children had managed to remove a good deal of mortar from cracks about a foot apart all up the wall, so now there was no difficulty in finding a sufficient resting-place for their feet. This was much lighter work than dragging heavy branches across the field from the wood-pile, and had consequently been more popular with everybody. But at last Madge had been obliged to remind her little band of labourers that even the best sort of staircase, if it led nowhere, was not very serviceable. So then they began to drag branches again, and very weary work they found it. And now at the end of a fortnight there were only five rough misshapen logs pulled up into the right place, with a great many torn pocket-handkerchiefs to show what a hard struggle it had been to lift them from the ground. No wonder John was becoming faint-hearted.

"You talked about a house big enough to hold several people, with a nice roof in case it rained," he said reproachfully.

Madge represented that it so seldom rained in June they could easily wait for their roof a little longer. "One can put that on at any time," she urged. "There is a good bough above, and we could spread an old shawl over it like a tent, or we might make a sort of wren's nest with sticks all up the sides and top, and crawl in through a hole. That would be very cozy, only I am afraid it would take a good many sticks, and you none of you like getting sticks."

"No, I don't," said John stoutly. "I've dragged enough of those old things across the field, and I won't be bothered with them any more. And it's no good talking about making it like a wren's nest—silly little birds that never fight or anything! What do eagles want with those sort of stuffy little houses?"

When John embarked on a thoroughly unreasonable grumble, it was no good arguing with him or interrupting him until he stopped from sheer loss of breath. So while he went on fault-finding, Madge was making up her mind to a great resolve. When at last he came to an end, she spoke out so decidedly that the twins were compelled to listen to her.

"Do you want to make the Eagle's Nest a great success—much the nicest thing we have ever done, or do you want to give it up altogether?" she inquired sternly.

"Not give it up! Of course, not give it up!" cried the two younger ones.

"Very well. I'm glad you said that. It would be a very cowardly and stupid thing to give it up when we have gone so far, but you can do just as you like."

"I never wanted to give it up," began John, in an injured tone; "only I don't want—"

"Well, if we are going on with it, I have quite settled what we will do," interrupted Madge briskly. "We will work away as hard as we can at it all the afternoon, and then whatever state it is in when the tea-bell rings we will declare it finished for the present, and begin to use it to play in. Of course, we can improve it as much as we like after, but we won't go on working any more just at present."

This suggestion met with general approval, for though the children had not at first minded the hard work of dragging branches from the wood-stack, now that much the same thing had been going on for a fortnight, they were getting rather tired of it and beginning to want a change. But after Madge's sensible proposal they worked away with all their first energy for the next two hours, and by the time the distant sounds of the tea-bell were heard across the fields, a very nice little platform had been built in the tree.

"I don't know what anybody could want better!" cried Madge, clapping her hands in high glee. "We will open it on Monday afternoon."

"It looks pretty open now without any walls or ceiling," observed John, who was always a little contradictory.

"Of course I mean open it as the Prince of Wales opens a hospital," Madge said with dignity.

"I know that well enough! You needn't always think I'm so stupid!" growled John.

This kind of conversation took place several times a day, but seldom ended in a real quarrel unless the children were rather tired or cross. To-day they were fortunately all in capital spirits at having finished their great work.

It seemed long to wait until Monday afternoon. But at last the time passed, and they were all standing together under the great beech-tree, with Madge explaining how the opening ceremony was to be performed.

"We will ascend the grand staircase," she said, "and standing in the assembly-room, the president (that's me, you know) will declare the buildings to be solemnly opened for public use."

This certainly sounded very well, though nobody knew exactly what it meant. The fact was that Madge repeated certain sentences she had read in newspapers, without troubling very much about the meaning.

"And when you've done that what shall we do?" inquired John.

"Well, if you can't think of anything to play when you have got into the Eagle's Nest you had better stay in the nursery and play with Baby," said Madge scornfully.

"Let us begin to ascend directly, and then we shall have more time for playing," interposed Betty, intent on keeping the peace.

"The president leads the way, of course!" exclaimed Madge, planting her toe in one of the niches of the wall. "I suppose both of you are obliged to use all the steps," she added carelessly. "I am so tall that I can stretch two at a time."

"So can I!" chimed in John; "it's only Betty who can't reach. Just get out of the way and I'll show you what I can do."

He immediately lifted his foot to the level of his chin, grabbed wildly at a projecting stone far above his head, missed it, and fell heavily on his back in a tuft of sting-nettles.

There was a good deal of confusion. Both the girls very kindly tried to help their brother up, and were naturally rather indignant when he hit out wildly at them, under the mistaken impression that they had pushed him down. Then they all stung their hands, and there was a long argument about who ought to have cleared the sting-nettles away from under the tree. But the simple idea of making up for past neglect by doing it now did not occur to any of them.

At last Madge recalled them all to their senses by declaring that she saw old Barton, the farm-man, in the distance, carrying the milk-pails. Though he was two fields off there could be no mistake, because he kept the pails so brightly polished that they glittered like diamonds in the sun. And he never started to milk the cows until the stable clock had struck four, so his appearance was a positive proof that the afternoon was passing rapidly by.

"I say, it's nearly tea-time! And I thought we had only just finished dinner! I do believe holiday afternoons are much shorter than others!" exclaimed John.

He was so overcome by this discovery that he allowed Madge to mount the grand staircase without interruption. But she did not avail herself of the rare chance of making a dignified welcoming speech to the younger ones as they climbed up behind her, for at that moment she was seized by a new idea of such importance that she was almost choked with anxiety to impart it at once to the others.

"This building is open!" she shouted impatiently. "And come on quickly, you two! I want to tell—"

"That's not the way people open things!" interrupted John. "It takes a much longer time than that. You ought to say its name, and make a speech about what it will be used for. Oughtn't she, Betty?"

Betty said nothing. She made a general rule of backing up her elder sister in family disputes, and yet she could not help feeling that in this case John had a just cause of complaint. The ceremony had been very disappointing.

"Very well then," said Madge, seeing that it was no use to fight against public opinion, "I suppose I must do it all over again. Although I have something to say that you can't even imagine."

"I don't believe there is such a thing," said John stolidly. "I can imagine anything a girl can, I know that."

Old as she was, Madge nearly cried with impatience. "If you are going to contradict and argue," she began, "it's no good—"

"We will be quiet! We will really!" interrupted Betty, who, on the whole, had a peace-loving disposition.

"Very well then," said Madge, recovering herself a little, but still speaking with rather terrific dignity. "I declare this Eagle's Nest open. It has been erected regardless of trouble and expense by—by—"

"The young eagles," suggested Betty.

"Yes, by the young eagles," continued Madge, "for the use and amusement of—of—"

"The young eagles," again suggested Betty.

"Of course! Amusement of the young eagles," repeated Madge rather inattentively, for she was thinking of something else. "And we hope they will enjoy it! And I think that's all. Now I'll tell you my last plan!"

"All right!" muttered John, settling himself with a contented grunt upon the sticks. Now that the new building had been properly opened, his mind was at rest.

"Well, this is what I think," began Madge. "It's rather absurd for us to have a grand staircase up to our place of refuge. What we want is a ladder that we can pull up after us so that the enemy can't follow!"

"What a splendid idea!" said Betty admiringly. "But I am afraid Barton would never allow us to take his ladders out of the barn. He is always dreadfully cross if we only take them out to look at a bird's nest, and he finds they have gone. And he would be sure to see us carrying them across the fields."

"Yes, but you see I have thought of all that!" replied Madge with a smile of superior wisdom. "I told you I had a good idea, and I have, though John did not believe it! What do you say to a rope-ladder?"

CHAPTER V
THE BOY WHO MOUNTED IT

It is just possible that there comes a time of life when the heart does not beat responsively at the bare suggestion of a rope-ladder. Then a desert island will have lost its charm, and wild beasts be no longer a source of terror or interest. Betty and John had, fortunately for them, not yet reached this miserable epoch. At their sister's last words they shouted and danced about on the uneven sticks until they were in imminent danger of falling out of the Eagle's Nest much faster than they climbed in.

"I thought you would consider it a good idea," said Madge modestly.

"Rather! I should think so! It's the awfullest, jolliest notion! It is! it is!" cried the twins alternately. At that moment they felt that nobody ever had ideas quite as good as Madge's.

But presently John, as usual, saw an objection to the scheme.

"I'm afraid string won't be strong enough," he began gloomily. "It might bear Betty's weight, but it certainly won't ours." He was at least two inches taller, and several pounds heavier than his twin sister, and was never tired of drawing attention to the fact.

"Do you think we are heavier than those great bundles of hay that Barton carries on his back when he is going to feed the cows in the winter?" inquired Madge.

John looked rather puzzled by this mysterious question, but Betty interposed hastily: "Oh, no! They must be much heavier than us! Why, Barton can sometimes hardly load them on his back and stoops almost double as he walks. And I know he can carry two of us, because one day when John and I were sitting on the pig-sty wall he came and just lifted us off one under each arm, and carried us all the way back to the garden as easily as possible."

"It wasn't because we were sitting on the pigsty wall that he lifted us off," observed John. "We are allowed to sit there as much as we like—at least you aren't, because it dirties your frocks, but I am. It was because you were throwing stones at the little pigs and he thought you would hurt them."

"It wasn't stones!" cried Betty indignantly. "It was little bits of moss I picked off the walls, because they had nothing green to eat—only—"

"Oh, children! Don't be so silly! Wrangling on about things that don't matter in the least!" interrupted Madge in her most sensible manner. "We all agree about the only thing of any consequence," she continued. "The ropes that go round the bundles of hay would be strong enough to bear us. And I know where to get them! They are coiled up behind the manger in the cow-house, and Barton has not used them lately as the cows are not having hay in the fields now."

After this speech the children naturally lost very little time in running to the cow-house. There, lying in a dark corner, were several coils of rope of unequal length, but all most reassuringly thick. They chose out two pieces that seemed as if they had been made on purpose to form the sides of a rope-ladder, and carried them off in triumph to the Eagle's Nest, feeling like a successful party of marauding barons in the middle ages. Just as they had hidden the rope in a fork of the beech-tree the bell for tea rang, and work was over for that afternoon. In warm weather, when the children strayed far from the house, Mrs. West had a large bell rung outside the door at meal-times, so there was really no excuse for not coming in. However, even with this precaution, Miss Thompson had so frequently to wait that she had lately made a rule to the effect that a quarter of an hour after the right time for tea to begin the cake and jam should be sent out of the room, and only bread and butter left. The children had been conspicuously more inclined to punctuality since this rule was made.

Everything connected with the Eagle's Nest took much more time and labour than was ever expected. It sounds an easy thing enough to make a rope-ladder when once the materials have been collected. But even with Barton's ropes, and Nurse's best ball of string, which John had quietly brought away in his pocket, it was no simple matter. After many days spent in faithfully following out all the directions given for the manufacture of rope-ladders in various books of adventures, the children produced something up which an intrepid traveller might possibly have crawled in preference to being eaten by a very hungry lion. With great pride they tied the upper ends of the two ropes firmly to a bough just above the Eagle's Nest. That part of the job was very effectually done. The children could be trusted to tie secure knots, they had such constant practice.

"Hurrah! Finished at last!" cried Madge, giving the ropes a severe jerk to test their firmness. "And now, who shall be the first to mount up our new ladder?"

"Let me!" cried a strange voice.

The children started so violently that they almost fell out of the Eagle's Nest. They looked all round in bewilderment, and at last, directly under the beech-tree, on the other side of the wall, they saw a boy watching them intently.

"If you will drop the end of the ladder down this way I know I can climb up," he said. "I've been looking at you for a long time, only you were so busy you didn't notice me. And I want to get up and have a look at that place you have built in the tree."

Betty and John turned to Madge and remained silent. The occasion was so strange that they gladly yielded to their elder sister the privilege of deciding what was to be done. But for once even the masterful Madge had some difficulty in making up her mind. There were so many things to be considered before taking any decisive action.

Of course it would be delightful to exhibit all their inventions and contrivances to a stranger, a boy who was apparently of an exact age to take an intelligent interest in such matters. But then, on the other hand, they had never been given permission to speak to this boy, and perhaps it was not the right thing to do.

"Still, I don't remember that we have ever been forbidden to talk to strangers, have we?" said Madge aloud. She was very anxious to be provided with an excuse for inviting this new boy to join the party.

"No, I don't think we have ever actually been told not to speak to people we don't know," said Betty thoughtfully. "But then, you know, Mama and Miss Thompson would never think of our meeting a stranger in the fields, and of course we don't go on the roads by ourselves."

This was perfectly true, but it did not suit Madge at all.

"I don't know what people think," she said impatiently; "only what they say. And if we have never been forbidden to speak to a stranger, I expect there is no harm in it. We are forbidden things fast enough if they are wrong. Sometimes it seems as if there would be hardly anything left that we are allowed to do!" She spoke rather recklessly, having half made up her mind to do something that she knew perfectly well was not right, and hoping by talking very loud and fast to stifle the voice of her conscience.

"You are keeping me a precious long time waiting!" called out the boy from below. "You don't mean to say you are such a set of babies that you are afraid to let down the ladder for me without first running back to the nursery to ask permission?"

At this taunt Madge became very red. "I've got nothing to do with the nursery, and I'm not afraid of anybody!" she exclaimed. These bold statements were not only silly but untrue; however, she did not stop to think of that in her overwhelming hurry to convince this stranger that she was not a little child, as he seemed to think, but a big girl with a will of her own. "And just to show you that I needn't trouble about anybody's permission, I invite you to join us up here," she added.

"That's right! You are a good sort, I can see!" returned the boy. "Drop down that old ladder of yours, and I will be with you in a couple of seconds! Now, look sharp, you two little ones. Lend a hand with the rope, can't you! What's the good of staring at me like two stuffed owls?"

To say the truth, Betty and John were both rather frightened by Madge's daring behaviour. They were by no means better children than she was, but they seldom ventured to be naughty on such a large scale as this. When Madge's pride was once roused she never stopped to think of consequences; but it is only fair to add, that being the eldest she generally same in for the largest share of punishment if they all did wrong together.

"Is he really coming up the ladder to play with us?" muttered Betty rather breathlessly in her sister's ear. "Do you think we shall be allowed—"

"Here, you parcel of babies, get out of the way!" interrupted the boy. "You've got nothing to do with it. Just chuck me down the rope," he added to Madge, "and if the babies don't like it they can run home and play in the nursery. We don't want them interfering with us! Rather not!"

Madge could not resist this flattering appeal. She did so enjoy being treated as a person of some importance, and not classed with the little ones. "Here goes!" she cried defiantly, and taking hold of the rope-ladder she dropped the end of it over the wall.

There was an anxious struggle. The strange boy appeared very active, for though one or two of the short sticks that formed the rungs of the ladder slipped (for it was almost impossible to tie them securely to the rope sides), yet he clung on with hands and feet like a monkey. When he came within reach Madge stooped down and stretched out her hand to him.

"Welcome to Eagle's Nest!" she said proudly, as she pulled him up to her side in the tree.

CHAPTER VI
A VICTIM

"So this is what you call Eagle's Nest?" cried the new-comer. "What a rum place!"

"It's a fortress," observed Madge with considerable dignity, for she did not quite like the want of respect with which he was criticising their great achievement. "It is only accessible by a rope-ladder and one other—" She stopped suddenly, thinking that after all it might not be wise to confide all their secrets to a stranger until he proved himself worthy of confidence.

"Oh, you needn't trouble to tell me," replied the boy; "I shall find it out quickly enough. I find out everything. I found you out playing up in this tree, though you couldn't see me."

"We did not know there were any children on the other side of the wall, so we didn't look particularly," explained Madge. "We thought an old lady lived—"

"Old Mother Howard you mean?" interrupted the boy. "Yes, she lives there right enough. And a rum old woman she is too!"

"Is she your mother, then?" asked John, rather puzzled by this speech.

"Rather not! I should jolly well like to see her dare to be my mother!" said the boy indignantly. "I'm an orphan, and she says she is some relation and has a right to bring me up. But I'll tell you something,"—he lowered his voice mysteriously, and the others crept a little nearer to him,—"it's my belief she is only trying to get all my money!"

"How dreadful!" exclaimed Madge. "I didn't know that people really did that sort of thing nowadays."

"Oh, don't they just!" said the boy, seemingly delighted by the impression his words had produced. "I'll just tell you how she has treated me. My father was a very rich man and I am his only child, so of course I ought to be rich, oughtn't I? Well, I hardly ever have any pocket-money at all!"

"We have threepence a week," said Betty with justifiable pride. But a moment later she was sorry that she had appeared to boast of their superior good fortune.

"Threepence a week! Do you indeed? But I dare say you have everything you want directly you ask for it?" observed the boy very dolefully. "What should you say if you had been left an orphan at the mercy of a cruel guardian, who sent you first to a school where they starved you, then to a school where they beat you, and then here where they do both?"

"Do you mean that Mrs. Howard starves and beats you?" inquired Madge, horrified by these disclosures.

"Oh, rather! Dry bread for dinner, and if you won't eat it you are locked up in the cellar until you do. It's quite dark, and the black beetles crawl over you. Ugh! Have you ever had a black beetle walk across your face?"

"No!" exclaimed Madge; "I've never touched one. Cook says she sometimes sees them on the kitchen floor at night, but of course we are in bed then."

"Well, think of being shut up in a perfectly dark cellar—"

"Is it underground?" interrupted John.

"Jolly well underground I should say!" continued the boy. "Fifty steps down, and an iron door at the top and the bottom of the stairs, so that however much you shouted nobody could possibly hear you. And nothing but slimy black earth to lie upon."

"How do you know it's black if you are in the dark?" asked Betty, so deeply interested in this terrible tale that she wished to understand every detail.

"I tell you I know it is black!" said the boy sharply. "Black, and covered with pools of dirty water. And there are toads all about. If you don't believe me, though, I won't tell you any more about it."

"Oh, I do believe you! It wasn't that at all," said Betty. "But what a dreadful woman Mrs. Howard must be! Jane says the village people think she is quite mad."

"And who is Jane?"

"She is our nurse-maid. But everybody thinks the same. Very likely Father and Mother do, only they never talk about Mrs. Howard to us."

"I dare say she is mad," said the boy. "I can tell you enough things about her to make your hair stand on end, although I have only been here a week."

"But how did you come here, and what is your name? And how old are you?" asked Madge.

"My name is Lewis Brand, and I was fourteen last Christmas."

"Then you are two years older than me!" cried Madge, this announcement putting everything else out of her head. "I had no idea you were so old as that. And you have been at school?"

"Two schools, and now I have been sent to prison here."

"I shall go to school soon," interposed John, who was rather ashamed of his want of experience before this big boy. John had been kept at home a little longer than would otherwise have been the case, because his mother had a romantic idea that the twins were inseparable. It had lately become apparent, however, that John and Betty were most affectionate when they did not see too much of each other; and since a baby-boy had lately appeared in the nursery, Captain West had felt that his eldest son could be very well spared to go to school.

"Ah, school is bad enough!" said Lewis gloomily. "You wait till you get there! You'll just jolly well wish you were home again! But," he broke off suddenly, "do let us begin to play. Talking all the afternoon is dull work."

It was wonderful how soon the victim of Mrs. Howard's cruelties recovered his spirits when they once started a game. He established himself as chief of a tribe of wild Indians, with the modest title "Bravest of the Brave". And he led his warriors to victory with such shrill battle-cries that the veriest coward would have felt compelled to follow him. The absence of enemies was the chief want that afternoon. They had to pretend that some iron railings on the other side of the field were an army advancing towards them in the distance.

"But it is much more fun when the enemy is alive, so that he runs away and we can hurt him," explained Madge. "Next time we will try to drive the pigs up to this end of the field when we are coming here. They make capital enemies, they scream so beautifully while they are running away."

It seemed to be taken for granted by everybody that in future Lewis would often join the three Wests in their games.

"And I'm sure Mama won't mind your coming to play with us when she hears how cruelly you are treated at home," observed Betty.

"You don't mean to say you were going to tell anybody that you met me here!" cried Lewis excitedly. "Now, that's just like a girl! They never can keep the least bit of a secret. If you say a single word about me to anybody at all I shall never be able to come here any more. And very likely something dreadful will happen to me."

"But Mama would not tell Mrs. Howard if I asked her not. Besides, she doesn't even know her," argued Betty, who was rather frightened at the prospect of keeping such a very large secret for an indefinite period.

"I tell you I shall be put in that dark cellar, and fed—" Lewis suddenly broke off, and whispered in a tone of real terror, "Lie down flat! Keep still! There she is!"

All four children happened to be on the Eagle's Nest at the moment, having just returned from a most violent raid against the Iron-Railing tribe, which, however, did not seem in any hurry to avenge its wrongs by pursuing the enemy back to his stronghold. At Lewis's words they all crouched down on the sticks, making themselves as small as possible. And they looked in the direction to which he silently pointed.

From the height of the Eagle's Nest it was possible to see over the boundary wall into Mrs. Howard's domain. It is a fact, however, that until to-day the children had found this view exceedingly uneventful. At the bottom of the wall there was a small orchard, beyond that a glimpse could be caught of an old-fashioned garden and the end of a brick house. It was all very ordinary and homely-looking, not at all like the surroundings one naturally expects to find associated with deeds of wrong and cruelty. But since the children had heard of the fearful cellar beneath that innocent brick house, they shuddered as they glanced towards it. And to-day for the first time they saw someone moving about the garden.

"Lie still," whispered Lewis, "as still as death! She is coming this way!"

Full of mingled terror and curiosity, Madge, Betty, and John lay motionless, hardly moving an eyelid. It was Lewis who fidgeted decidedly the most, in spite of his having been the one to give the order for silence. And presently through a gate from the garden came an old lady. She was dressed all in gray—gown, shawl, and bonnet, and most delicately clean and neat she looked. In her hand she carried a nosegay of white flowers, and a few paces behind her solemnly stalked a large black cat.

There were only two remarkable things about this old lady's appearance—always excepting her extreme air of daintiness. One was the smallness of her size, the other her funny trick of nodding her head continually. The latter seemed as much a habit with her as breathing; she nodded at the buttercups and daisies beneath her feet, and she nodded at the two sleek cows, who stopped chewing the cud for a moment to gaze back with blinking, white-lashed eyes. She even nodded more than once towards the beech-tree, until Madge made sure that they were discovered, and began to prepare a fine speech, defying Mrs. Howard to trespass one inch on Captain West's land. But after all there was no opportunity for delivering this timely warning, as the old lady glided slowly on through the orchard, and having gently inspected (and nodded to) every individual apple-tree, she returned to the garden and disappeared round a corner of the house, closely followed by the black cat.

"So that's Mrs. Howard!" exclaimed Madge, stretching her cramped limbs after the effort of remaining still so long. "She doesn't look as if she could hurt you very much. Why, I don't believe she is as tall as I am!"

"Perhaps not," replied Lewis. "But I never said she shut me up herself, did I? She keeps a sort of jailer to do that. And she stands and grins on the top step while he is hurling me into the cellar below. You should see her grin!"

"But she looks so gentle," objected Betty.

"I'll tell you the reason of that. It's to deceive people and get them into her clutches," said Lewis. "Now I must be off, or they will half-murder me if they find out where I have been. I'll try and come another day if I can give old Mother Howard the slip." And seizing the rope-ladder, which had been hidden among the branches, he again dropped it over the wall. Climbing down the ladder was a much quicker matter than climbing up, and in a couple of minutes he was safely running across the orchard towards the brick house.

CHAPTER VII
JACK AND JILL

When Lewis Brand had disappeared from sight, the three children left in the Eagle's Nest could scarcely believe that since dinner-time so many curious things had happened. A strange boy, of whose existence they were not aware two hours before, had been playing with them just as if they had known each other all their lives. He had, moreover, told them his history, which was quite as wonderful as many fairy stories. And they had seen the mysterious Mrs. Howard.

These extraordinary new experiences had the effect of quite throwing the rope-ladder into the background, and they actually forgot all about its existence, and descended by the wall in the old way at the warning sound of the tea-bell. John was the first to notice this omission.

"Oughtn't we to climb up again and come down by the ladder?" he said.

"Oh no, bother the ladder!" replied Madge, so curtly that the others stared at her in surprise.

"But the ladder was your idea, your very own idea. And I thought you were so proud of it!" observed Betty in a bewildered voice.

"Oh yes, so I was!" cried Madge impatiently. "But don't you see, so many new things have happened that they have nearly put the old things out of my head. The ladder is quite safe up there twisted round the bough. Barton will never think of looking in the tree even if he does miss it, but it's my belief he doesn't count the ropes all through the summer. Now let us hurry back or there will be a fuss about our keeping tea waiting, and we sha'n't be allowed to go so far away in the fields. You know Miss Thompson once threatened not to let us out of sight of the schoolroom window if we so often came in late."

On the way home Madge impressed upon the other two the necessity of not boasting of their adventure.

"Mayn't we even say that we have seen Mrs. Howard? Not even tell Jane?" they asked.

"Certainly not," said Madge sternly. "It is not our own secret, remember. It is Lewis's. And we have promised him to say nothing about it, so of course we mustn't."

When the case was put that way it certainly sounded right to hold one's tongue. And yet a little time before it had seemed equally right to go home and confess that they had taken the unusual step of talking to a stranger. The younger ones couldn't help feeling that this was very confusing. Besides, it was disappointing to be forbidden to tell Jane that they now knew more about Mrs. Howard even than she did.

They would have discussed the subject all the way home if the sight of Captain West coming to meet them across the fields had not given an entirely new turn to their thoughts. As soon as they came near enough to hear what he said he shouted out:

"Come along quickly! I have been looking for you ever since I came back from Churchbury. There is a surprise for you!"

There was nothing the children liked better than being with their father. He was away a great part of every day attending Magistrates' meetings, Boards of Guardians, and other useful county work. When he came home late in the afternoon, Madge, Betty, and John made such a rush for him that Mrs. West often complained that she could not get any attention until the children had gone to bed. It was no use her trying to talk, she said, every word was drowned by the three loud voices that insisted upon being heard and answered.

At the bare mention of a surprise the children set off running. They knew of old that their father's surprises usually meant a new toy or something good to eat. As they rushed up to him he quietly stepped on one side, and they all three rolled over in a heap.

"That was a fine escape for me," laughed Captain West. "If I hadn't been on the look-out you would have knocked me over too, I suppose. No, I will not be pawed by six dirty hands! There's nothing in my pocket, I tell you!"

"But you said there was a surprise!" panted John, who had not been able to run quite as fast as his sisters, and consequently had fallen on the top of the heap and was the first to rise.

"Quite true! But all surprises aren't made of chocolate, and don't live in my pocket as you seem to think," replied Captain West. "This one came from America. Now guess what it is?"

"But we can't!" shouted three despairing voices. "Oh, please tell us! Do tell us!"

"Nonsense! A little thinking strengthens the mind," said Captain West calmly. "You all learn geography. Now what comes from America?"

"Christopher Columbus!" screamed Betty, who was in such a hurry to answer first that she had not listened very attentively to the question.

"Very well. I promise that if he comes you shall have him all to yourself," observed her father.

"Oh, I didn't mean that! Let me try again!" cried the little girl, who had just discovered from the laughter of the others that she had said something rather foolish.

"No, no! You have had your turn, and if you didn't listen I can't help it. What do you say, Madge?"

"Corn, cotton, india-rubber—"

"Oh, stop! That will do. I don't want the whole geography-book from end to end. What do you say, John?"

"I say the same as the others," replied John, who did not take the trouble to think on his own account, and fancied this statement must be safe.

"What!" cried Captain West, pretending to be much alarmed at the news; "you really think Christopher Columbus and all the products of North and South America have come as a little surprise to us? This is very overpowering. Before proceeding any further in my investigations I shall certainly require some tea to strengthen me;" and he started off walking rapidly towards the house.

"Papa! That's too bad! We can't eat any tea until we know what it is!" they all shouted.

"I am sorry for that," said Captain West coolly; "because I happen to be very hungry, as I only had a biscuit for lunch at Churchbury. It will be rather dull work watching me, I am afraid."

At this moment Mrs. West appeared at the drawing-room window, holding up a cup as a signal to her husband that his tea was ready. He hurried towards her immediately, telling the children that he should be ready in a quarter of an hour. So there was nothing for it but to wash their hands and run to the schoolroom, where they arrived just in time to save the jam, which was in the very act of being carried out of the room. And after all, in spite of their excitement, they contrived to make a very good tea, for it was a long time since dinner, and they had hardly been still for a moment.

Mrs. West was not very strong, so that she had to spend a great deal of the day on the sofa, and could seldom join in the children's out-door amusements.

But this surprise from America was so exceptionally interesting that she declared she must come out and see it; so, with a shawl carefully tied round her, she accompanied her husband and children to the stables after tea.

"Take care!" cried Captain West, with his hand on the latch of one of the stable doors; "take care it doesn't jump out!"

"Is it alive? Can it run? Will it bite?" asked the children in astonishment.

But before they had time to say more the door was opened, and they caught sight of two most graceful little goats shrinking timidly into a corner.

"Are they for us?" inquired Madge, in a wondering tone of voice; for, so far, they had never owned anything larger than a pet rabbit, and the idea of having these beautiful goats for their own seemed almost too good to be true.

"They are absolutely your property," said Captain West. "I have nothing to do with them at all, except that I suppose I shall have the honour of paying for what they eat and break."

"Oh, Papa! They look much too dainty to break anything with their tiny little hoofs," said Madge reproachfully. "And I can see they will eat very little. But how do you think we had better divide two between three of us?"

"There are several ways," replied her father. "You might have the heads, Betty the bodies, and John the tails."

But this suggestion did not give entire satisfaction.

"If Madge wanted to feed her heads in the stable just when I had my bodies out walking on the road, how should we manage?" asked Betty.

"That is indeed a difficult question to decide," said Captain West thoughtfully. "I see that it is a much more difficult matter to keep goats than I had ever imagined. Perhaps after all it would be safer to send them back to America?"

"Oh, no! But I see you don't mean it!" cried Madge. "You are only joking."

"I don't know about that," said her father. "It isn't a very joking matter. One of my old friends who has been lately travelling about America just writes to say that he has brought back a charming pair of little goats, and as he can't keep them in his London house he is sending them as a present to my children. He might have consulted me first, I think, especially as the goats arrived a few hours after the letter."

"Oh, but you wouldn't have stopped them? They are such darlings!" cried Madge. "They won't give any trouble, and they will draw a little cart."

"Well, they look rather wild for that kind of work at present," observed Captain West; "but I dare say they will grow tamer. And as they are here I suppose I must make the best of them, as I do of wasps and rats."

"How can you compare them to such nasty things?" demanded Madge indignantly. "Although I know you only do it to tease us! And now we must think of names. That is always so hard, because we can never quite agree about names. The white mice all died before we could make up our minds what to call them."

"Then I am thankful to say the poor goats will be saved from that fate," said her father. "My friend expressly says that they have names. They are called Jack and Jill!"

CHAPTER VIII
AN EARLY CHASE

The excitement of the goats' arrival quite put all thoughts of Lewis Brand and his wonderful story out of the children's heads. Fortunately the evenings were light and long, for there was a great deal to be done before the two pets could be considered safely housed for the night. Captain West objected to their remaining any longer in the stables as he could not spare the room, so there was a great discussion about where they could be shut up for the night. At last it was decided that a railed-off corner of the cow-house, where calves generally lived, would be very suitable, and in the daytime, of course, they could be loose in the fields with the other animals. As they seemed rather wild, it was safer to shut them up at night for fear of their wandering away. So the children were at last persuaded to leave them for the night, with a plentiful supply of fresh grass, in case they should wake and feel hungry.

"What a lot of things have happened to-day!" exclaimed Betty when she and Madge were both in bed, and Jane had left the room with her usual piece of good advice to them to go to sleep at once. Two children occupying beds in the same room were not very likely to take such a sensible piece of advice, and in point of fact Madge and Betty often talked away merrily for a long time. "Sometimes it seems as if nothing happened for weeks, and to-day there are so many things I can hardly remember them all," continued Betty. "Doesn't it seem a long time since we let down the rope-ladder and that boy climbed into the Eagle's Nest?"

"Yes. But do be quiet, I want to go to sleep," said Madge rather crossly. She had been feeling so much happier since she had quite forgotten Lewis Brand and the difficulties connected with him, that she was not at all grateful for having the whole affair brought back to her mind again.

But Betty could not leave the subject alone. "Do you think Lewis is a nice boy?" she inquired. "I didn't like him at first, because he has such a white face and hardly any eyebrows!"

"What a silly reason for not liking a person," said Madge. "As if they could help their eyebrows!"

"I know it's silly," returned Betty humbly. "But don't you find it very difficult to like people when they have nasty faces?"

"I never think about their faces," said Madge in a superior way. "If they are jolly I like them soon enough, however ugly they are!"

"Oh, so do I!" exclaimed Betty, now rather ashamed of her criticisms as she found that Madge considered them silly. "At first I thought he was going to be rather proud and stuck-up because he was so much older than we are, but afterwards he seemed very nice when we began to play. I wonder if we shall ever see him again?"

"I'm sure I don't know! Let us go to sleep now, I'm tired of talking;" and Madge burrowed so deeply under the bed-clothes that it was quite impossible to carry on any sort of conversation with her.

Perhaps it was because Madge went to sleep rather early that evening that she was enabled to wake proportionately early the following morning. It was fairly light and fine, though not sunny. She got out of bed and went to the window. Madge invariably looked out of the window the first thing in the morning, but to-day she was rewarded by seeing something that had never met her eyes before.

On the lawn, directly in front of the house, was a large flower-bed, containing many roses of different colours. They were Mrs. West's favourite flowers, and even when she could not go out, she enjoyed seeing them from the drawing-room window. In the middle of this flower-bed now stood Jack and Jill, cropping off and devouring dozens of rose-buds with evident relish.

Madge rubbed her eyes and looked again. It was no dream, and there was no possibility of a mistake. She had seen the goats safely shut into the calves' house the night before, and here they were loose and walking about the garden. She could not understand in the least how it had happened; but nevertheless it was a fact. And, moreover, they were eating her mother's favourite roses as fast as they could. She tapped gently on the window-pane, but the goats took absolutely no notice. At this rate there would not be a rose left by the time the gardener came to work.

A great idea occurred to Madge. We know that she was rather independent, as befitted the eldest of a family, and decidedly fond of managing things her own way. So it presently came about that she decided not to let the roses be eaten, and not to disturb anybody else, but to drive Jack and Jill out of the garden all by herself. Perhaps it seemed rather unkind not to wake Betty, who was sleeping quietly in her little bed in the other corner of the room. However, she looked so comfortable that it was almost a pity to disturb her, and after all she was two years younger than Madge, and could not reasonably expect to do exactly the same things as her elder sister. She would be very full of reproaches when she woke up, but Madge resolved to risk a little sisterly abuse sooner than permit anyone to share the glory of her exploit.

It really does not take very long to dress if one omits all ornamental additions, and dispenses with everything in the shape of a bath! Jack and Jill had not time to do more than taste the succulent young shoots of half a dozen rose-trees before Madge had crept downstairs and quietly opened the front-door. Then with a half-suppressed shout of battle she rushed towards them, waving a walking-stick which she had the presence of mind to snatch up in passing through the hall. The goats both gave a guilty start at the first sound, and then crossed the lawn in a series of most amazing bounds. Madge afterwards compared them to gigantic grasshoppers; and, indeed, as she panted hopelessly behind them, she would scarcely have felt surprised if one of her nimble pets had, with a higher leap than usual, suddenly perched on the bough of a tree or the roof of a house!

Madge had often laughed at her father's little terrier, Snap, for chasing the sparrows up and down the lawn in the vain hope of some day catching them, but she soon began to realize that she had started on quite as hopeless an enterprise herself. However rapidly she ran along the paths, however stealthily she stalked behind the bushes, Jack and Jill proved quicker and more artful. When, with untold trouble, she had driven them into a corner, and was advancing with outstretched hands to grasp their pert little horns, they would just toss their heads, and without any apparent effort skip right over her shoulder and be off half across the garden almost before she could turn round.

"I do believe I shall have to go back and fetch Betty after all," muttered Madge, when this sort of thing had gone on so long that she was fairly tired out. "Not that she can run half as fast as I can, her legs are so short! But she could help. I really can't be expected to do all the work by myself!"

Madge was getting tired, and consequently cross. So, rather funnily, she was beginning to feel it quite a grievance that nobody had come out to help her to drive the goats, forgetting that it was entirely her own wish to undertake the job alone. As she somewhat sullenly walked towards the house, she prepared several severe speeches to be addressed to Betty on the selfishness of lying in bed and leaving her sister to do all the work. But just as she was getting into a state of considerable indignation, out of the open front-door walked her father.

Captain West had evidently dressed in a hurry like his daughter. In point of fact he had been suddenly wakened by one of Madge's involuntary cries, for though she had every intention of being very quiet, she could not altogether suppress an occasional shout when the goats were unusually irritating. He had started up and looked into the passage. All seemed quiet, but a gleam of light in the hall below showed him that the front-door was open. Between three and four o'clock in the morning this was a fairly peculiar circumstance. So, returning to his room he hastily slipped on the first clothes he came across and proceeded downstairs, to find out who was about at that early hour.

"Hullo, Madge! What on earth are you doing?" he exclaimed, as he suddenly found himself face to face with his eldest daughter.

Madge explained the whole story in rather a confused, disjointed sort of way. It was not at all the triumphal return to the house that she had planned. If things had gone as she intended she would easily have caught Jack and Jill; they would have come to eat a little grass out of her hand, and then she would gently but firmly have led them back to the calves' house. Here she would have secured the door more skilfully than her elders had done the previous evening, so that there would have been no further possibility of escape for the prisoners. And then she would have strolled quietly back to the house, and explained to an admiring audience at breakfast-time what precautions she had taken for the safety of the garden while the more negligent members of the family slept. It was certainly very disappointing to be treated by her father as a naughty child instead of a heroine, and scolded for her stupidity in running out on the wet grass in thin shoes.

"But I couldn't expect it to be wet in the summer," replied Madge, who would seldom admit that she was in the wrong without an argument.

"Don't talk nonsense!" said Captain West severely. He would play with the children all day, and readily forgive them any damage they did through carelessness, but he never could stand their trying to argue that wrong was right. "You know as much about dew as I do," he continued; "and I have put on thick boots while you have been running about for an hour in dripping wet shoes."

It was quite impossible to deny this, for Madge's feet presented a most miserable appearance. She had been running through the shrubberies, where the long wet grass reached up to her knees, and her kid shoes were also scratched and muddy.

"If I go in and put on thick boots may I come out again and help you to drive the goats?" inquired Madge anxiously.

Seeing how very wet she was, Captain West did not dare grant this request, but ordered her straight back to bed. With many a grumble Madge returned to her room and threw all her clothes in a heap on the floor. Then she slowly climbed into bed, protesting to herself that she should be sure to lie awake until it was time to get up, in spite of which resolve she fell asleep in about two minutes.

Whether Jack and Jill thought that Captain West did not look like a person to be trifled with, or whether they were really getting a little tired of their prolonged frolic, it is impossible to say. At all events, soon after he appeared they allowed themselves to be quietly driven to the end of the garden and out through the door into the farmyard, where they remained until Barton came to milk the cows in the morning.

CHAPTER IX
AN ALARMING JUMP

"I'll tell you what it is, children," said Captain West briskly as he entered the dining-room rather late for breakfast, "if these pets of yours are going to keep me trotting about the garden at night I shall lose my excellent character for punctuality in the morning. Why, here is Madge coming down late too, and looking very displeased with the world. I don't know if Jack and Jill are responsible for her frowns as well as my lateness; if so, they have a good deal upon their consciences!"

The fact of the matter was, that poor Madge was labouring under a grievance. In the morning she and Betty usually tried who should get down earliest to breakfast, and to-day, as might have been expected, Madge's shoes had shrunk up so uncomfortably after their wetting that she could not get them on without a great deal of rough handling. And then, to make matters worse, Nurse had declared that they were still damp, and made her take them off again to be put in front of the fire and thoroughly dried. Of course Betty was downstairs and half through a basin of bread-and-milk before Madge appeared, with a very gloomy countenance.

However, Captain West could not abide melancholy faces around the table, and he began to make such outrageous suggestions about a fitting punishment for the goats who had disturbed his night's rest, that at last even Madge was compelled to relax into a smile.

"Oh, don't pretend you will shave them, Papa! I don't believe anybody could make them stand still enough to be shaved," she said. "And as for harnessing them to the brougham, you know they are so small they would slip through the horses' great collars. But it would be very nice to have a tiny cart that they really could draw," she added wistfully.

"I think the first thing is to accustom your steeds to come when they are called," replied Captain West. "It will be very awkward if, whenever you want to go for a drive, you have to chase them up hill and down dale for an hour before you can catch them."

Acting on this suggestion, the children spent all their spare moments during the next day or two in trying to make friends with the goats. They were so successful, that at last Jack would consent to be led about by a bit of string tied to one of his horns, almost as quietly as a little dog. Jill remained shy to the last, and in spite of being perpetually offered the most tempting bits of carrot, could never summon up sufficient courage to eat anything out of the children's hands.

"Now that Jack is so tame he shall join in all our games," said Madge. So the children led him about everywhere with them in the garden and fields. But they never dared let go the string, or he would be off, running and leaping into the most extraordinary places before they could come up with him again.

Poor Barton was much perplexed where to shut up the two goats at night. The cow-house was a perfect failure; Jack and Jill stayed in it just as long as they liked, and not a moment longer. Unless all the doors and windows were shut, which was very stuffy in hot weather, there was no keeping them in an instant after they had decided to take a walk. And if they got out, they were not content to stay in the fields, but always found their way into the garden, where they cropped off the most cherished shrubs and flowers.

At last Barton hit on the plan of putting them into an empty pig-sty for the night and spreading a piece of old netting over the opening. This was very successful for a time.

When Jack was sufficiently tamed to be led about it occurred to the children that they might now introduce him to the Eagle's Nest. They had rather neglected their fortress of late, having had so much occupation at home with the goats; in fact they had not visited the beech-tree for nearly a week, not since the eventful day when they had seen Mrs. Howard and made acquaintance with Lewis Brand. In the new interest of training Jack and Jill everything else had been forgotten. But as they came near the Eagle's Nest all their old excitement in it revived.

"Will Jack have to walk up the grand staircase or the rope-ladder?" inquired John. "Or shall we have to lift him?"

"We can't stretch high enough to do that," observed Betty.

It was left to Madge as usual to decide this important question. She gave it as her opinion that with a little help from behind Jack could mount the grand staircase. "I will go up first," she said, "and pull at his horns. Then I can let down the rope-ladder for you two."

"I thought we left the rope-ladder coiled round that bough just above the Eagle's Nest," remarked Betty, "but I can't see it there now."

"Little Blind Eyes! Of course it must be there. I twisted it round the branch rather tightly, on purpose that it shouldn't show from below!" cried Madge rather impatiently, for she was leading Jack by a piece of string, and as he continually hung back to nibble bits of grass that looked especially tempting, it required a great deal of waiting about and coaxing to get along at all.

"I can't see it there now," repeated Betty obstinately.

"Oh, don't go on staring up at that old rope-ladder!" exclaimed Madge, "You just hold Jack at the bottom of the tree while I climb the grand staircase. And then, when I am ready to pull his horns, both push him from behind as hard as you can."

Whether Jack was more active even than they had credited him with being, or whether the twins pushed harder than had been expected, will never be known. At all events, long before Madge was firmly seated on the Eagle's Nest there was a terrific scramble, and the goat bounded past her almost knocking her out of the tree. In the struggle not to fall she very naturally dropped the leading-string and clung with both hands to a bough. Jack took advantage of his opportunity. Without pausing more than a second on the Eagle's Nest he skipped lightly on to the top of the boundary wall, and from there took a tremendous jump right into Mrs. Howard's orchard.

"He's gone!" shrieked Madge. "Oh, what shall we do!"

Quite overcome by this unforeseen calamity, the children actually forgot to quarrel among themselves about who was responsible for the accident. They all crouched down on the sticks composing the Eagle's Nest, and watched almost in silence the scene that was going on down in the orchard. At first Jack appeared frantic with delight at having regained his freedom and discovered a new playground. He scampered round and round the orchard, kicking up his heels, and disturbing horribly the placid old cows who were standing half asleep in the shade, chewing the cud and slowly whisking their tails to drive the flies off their sleek backs. But after a time it seemed as if Jack began to feel rather strange amidst his new surroundings. He left off frisking, and wandered restlessly about the orchard as if searching for some way to get out. Once or twice he looked up at the wall and bleated rather piteously.

"He wants to get back," said Betty. "Do you think he can possibly jump up the wall again?" She spoke almost in a whisper, having an uncomfortable feeling that if Mrs. Howard heard strange voices she might appear as suddenly as she had done on the last occasion.

"It's too high and straight even for Jack," replied Madge sadly. "You know the trunk of the tree helped him on this side, and, besides, you and John were both pushing him from behind."

"I've thought of a way," cried Betty. "Only I'm not quite sure whether I should dare to do it. I would, if you promised to come with me. It is for two of us to go down the rope-ladder into the orchard and try to catch Jack, and then—"

"Push him up the wall again, you mean?" interrupted Madge eagerly. "Yes, we'll do it! It's the only way we can get Jack back."

"But won't it be trespassing to go into Mrs. Howard's field?" inquired John.

This suggestion rather damped the spirits of the party. They knew that if you were caught trespassing, very terrible though ill-defined things might happen. When Barton found that village boys had been walking over the farm, searching for birds' nests and trampling down the mowing grass, he always said they had better not let him catch them trespassing or they would never forget it. He never condescended to explain exactly what punishment awaited them; but it sounded rather like imprisonment for life, with hard labour. So the little Wests grew up with a wholesome terror of being found trespassing, believing that such an offence might lead to something much more severe than the scolding at home, which was all the punishment they received for ordinary acts of mischief.

"Perhaps it would not count as trespassing if we stood on the rope-ladder," said Betty hopefully. "And Jack might come to us if we called him. Anyhow, we could climb up again quickly if we saw Mrs. Howard coming, and she could never say that we had been exactly on her land."

"I tell you what," said Madge after a moment's thought, "I shall go down the rope-ladder after Jack even if I have to run into the middle of the field to catch him. And if it's trespassing I can't help it. You two can sit in the Eagle's Nest and warn me if you see any danger. I would rather do it all by myself."

When Madge spoke in that decided kind of way, the younger ones knew that she had made up her mind. And they were justly proud of her bravery and energy. But an unexpected obstacle prevented Madge from carrying her heroic design into execution. When they began to search for the rope-ladder it was not there!

No doubt Madge had been perfectly correct in saying that she had left it safely coiled round a branch, the last time they played at the Eagle's Nest. Only Betty had been equally right as she crossed the field in saying that she could not see it there to-day. The children would probably have noticed its disappearance much sooner if they had not been so absorbed in watching Jack. There seemed really nothing left to be done; for even Madge with all her length of limb and daring courage could not get up or down a wall ten feet high without any help.

CHAPTER X
THE TRESPASSER

"Look! look!" exclaimed Betty suddenly, in a hoarse whisper. She pointed towards the orchard, and then crouched down behind a branch, trying to look even smaller than nature had made her. The others followed her example, until they were not much more conspicuous than three young squirrels. But though the children scarcely dared breathe in their anxiety to remain hidden, six eager eyes were strained towards a certain point in the orchard.

A tall, thin man, with a gray beard, was standing not many yards from Jack, carefully examining him through an eye-glass. How the man got there nobody knew; possibly he rose up from the earth or fell down from the sky; more probably he walked out of Mrs. Howard's garden gate while the children were hunting for their rope-ladder. At any rate he seemed immensely surprised at Jack's presence in the orchard.

A TALL, THIN MAN WAS CAREFULLY EXAMINING JACK

A TALL, THIN MAN WAS CAREFULLY EXAMINING JACK

The gray-bearded man stood irresolute for some time, as if unable to make up his mind exactly how to treat the intruder. At last he walked away towards the house, shouting to someone in the garden to come to his assistance. Presently in answer to his call a boy ran across the field. Even in the distance the children recognized that it was Lewis Brand, and they became if possible more interested in the proceedings than they were before.

With considerable difficulty the gray-bearded man and Lewis hunted Jack into a corner of the field, but just as they were about to catch the goat he invariably sprang past them and escaped. Madge could hardly keep from laughing aloud, because it was all so exactly what had happened to her when she tried to drive Jack and Jill out of the garden.

The Wests wondered a good deal if Lewis had any idea that the goat belonged to them, and whether he noticed them crouching in the beech-tree. For a long time he seemed absolutely unconscious of their presence, but suddenly, when the gray-bearded man's back was turned, Lewis looked towards the Eagle's Nest and unmistakably smiled. In a moment Madge had replied by waving her pocket-handkerchief frantically among the branches.

Instead of replying in a friendly spirit to this signal, Lewis made the most horrible grimace, put his finger to his lip, and turned away resolutely.

"We must keep very quiet. He is afraid of being seen," whispered Madge, putting her handkerchief away. But she could not help feeling rather mortified that Lewis had not trusted to her discretion only to wave when his companion was looking the other way. She was not in the habit of doing stupid things, and Lewis might have known it.

After a great deal of running up and down, the gray-bearded man seemed to consider it a hopeless task ever to catch Jack, so he changed his plan and tried to drive the goat into a little shed in the corner of the field. This was a much easier feat to accomplish, and in ten minutes more Jack was safely imprisoned and the door shut. Then the gray-bearded man, evidently much exhausted by his exertions, walked off to the garden, fanning himself with his black felt hat as he went. Lewis lingered behind his companion for one moment, and rapidly made a mysterious series of signs. First he pointed at the door of the shed where Jack was inclosed, then drew his hand across his own throat several times. Lastly he shook his fist violently at the back of the gray-bearded man as he followed him out of the field.

"What did Lewis mean by making all those funny faces?" asked John, when, the enemy being quite out of sight, the children dared once more speak and move.

"I don't know," said Madge. "It looked as if he were angry with that man—"

"No!" interrupted Betty. "It's worse than that! Lewis was trying to show us that the gray-bearded man is going to hurt poor Jack. I believe he has gone for a knife to cut his throat!"

There was a horrified silence after these words, for the more the children thought over them the more likely did it appear that Lewis's signs had really contained some such terrible meaning. Madge as usual was the first to come out with a heroic resolution.

"If that terrible man comes back with a knife to murder Jack," she said, "I shall jump off the wall and attack him with a stick. Very likely I shall break both my legs, but I don't care. I can't leave Jack to his fate."

Betty and John listened with uneasy admiration. They were just as sorry about Jack as Madge was; almost in tears at the idea of his possible death. But they did not feel brave enough to jump off the wall and risk breaking their legs. If it had been one leg between them perhaps they might have faced it, but four legs were too many for even brave twins to sacrifice.

"Why do you think you will break them both if you jump?" asked Betty anxiously, hoping against hope that there might be some miscalculation.

"Because I know you can break one leg if you only fall five or six feet, and this is double that height," replied Madge promptly.

Such logical reasoning did not admit of a single ray of hope.

"I don't think we are big enough to jump, then," said Betty modestly. And for once John did not contradict her.

However, for the second time that afternoon Madge was spared having to carry out a heroic resolve. The gray-bearded man did not return, either with or without a knife. It is true that Jack's voice could occasionally be heard raised in distressed accents from the inside of the shed. But unless his life was in imminent danger, even Madge did not feel inclined to sacrifice her limbs.

"After all, it was entirely his own fault jumping over the wall," she remarked when they had waited a long time without anything happening.

"And they don't seem to be going to kill him," observed Betty.

"And it's long past tea-time," added John.

This last consideration decided the children, and they returned to the house without taking any further steps towards rescuing Jack.

Nothing more was heard of the missing pet that evening. The children did not say anything about his escape, and their father happened to be staying out rather late, so that when he came home Barton had left work.

The old man had noticed that there was only one goat in the field when he went to drive them in for the night, but he did not waste much time hunting for Jack, having expressed his opinion from the first that it would be a good job when those nasty creatures either ran away or got sent off in disgrace! He did not like any pets, regarding them as useless creatures who ate food, gave trouble, and repaid nothing. If he had been allowed his way the children's tame rabbits and pigeons would all have gone into pies.

Of course there was a good deal of anxiety about Jack's fate among the only three people at Beechgrove who knew all the facts of his disappearance. As the hours passed by, and they actually went to bed and got up again without hearing any news, they began to wonder if, after all, they should never know what had become of him. When they all went to the schoolroom, and lessons began as usual, this really seemed rather probable. But in the middle of saying the English dates there was a knock at the door. John noticed it first, not because his hearing was particularly acute so much as on account of its being his turn to say the next date—which he had forgotten.

"Do attend, John!" said Miss Thompson. "Who came after Queen Anne? You always forget!"

"But there was a knock at the door, I am sure! Yes, there's another!" And for once John proved to be in the right, for at that moment Captain West entered the room.

"I'm dreadfully sorry to interrupt," he said to Miss Thompson, "for I can see by the children's faces that something very interesting is going on—"

"Oh, Papa!" interrupted Betty. "Why, it's only the English dates!"

"Well, what can be more interesting?" But as nobody answered he continued: "However, I haven't time to discuss the delights of your various studies, I must leave that to you and Miss Thompson to settle between you. All I want to say at present is, that you children must really be careful and not get me into trouble with my neighbours. I have just had a letter brought by Mrs. Howard's servant making complaints. Now mind, I can't have any more of this trespassing on—"

"We didn't step on Mrs. Howard's ground! Not one single inch!" interrupted Madge.

"I didn't ever suppose that you did, considering the height of the wall you would be obliged to climb over to get there!" said Captain West. "But there has been a trespasser on her land all the same, and I hold you partly responsible for him."

"Is it Jack?" gasped Madge. "What has she done with him? Oh, please tell me!"

"Why, sent him back, to be sure, with a polite note requesting me to keep him under better control," answered Captain West. "It seems that he got over the wall into her field somehow, and they shut him up for a time. But he got loose before long, as usual, and in chasing him about the garden some boy broke a cucumber-frame, and poor Jack got all the blame for that as well as for destroying a row of early peas. So he was sent back in sad disgrace."

"Did Mrs. Howard try to kill him?" asked John solemnly.

"Kill him? No!" laughed Captain West. "Did you think she wanted roast kid for dinner? But how did he manage to jump over such a high wall, I wonder? I suppose he did it while you were in the fields with him, as you seem to know all about it?"

"He jerked the string out of my hand and went off with it," said Madge.

"And jumped the wall, I suppose?" added her father. "Well, it's a tremendous height even for a goat, but one never can tell how high they will go. However, I mustn't interrupt you any more at lesson-time."

"This will teach Jack to look before he leaps," said Betty softly as the door shut behind her father. She always enjoyed having the last word, especially if she could twist it into a proverb.

The children were much relieved at this happy conclusion to their anxiety; but their delight was somewhat lessened when Captain West made a rule that Jack and Jill were never to be let out of their pig-sty unless he was at home to see that they did not get into mischief. The poor goats did not at all approve of remaining prisoners so much of their time; but really it seemed the only way of preventing them from breaking bounds. The children did what they could to cheer their pets in captivity by bringing them handfuls of cabbages and carrots at all hours in the day, and Jack and Jill began to grow so fat that before long it was to be hoped they would lose all taste for jumping.

CHAPTER XI
CERTAIN LITTLE GARDENS

It is wonderful how often grown-up people walk about the world with their eyes shut. Captain West thought himself decidedly an observant man. He was fond of his garden, and even worked in it for hours at a time; but he never noticed that within his domain there were sundry other little gardens, just as carefully tended, and exhibiting a much greater ingenuity of arrangement than his own. For instance, there was one within a few yards of the schoolroom window, just at the corner of the house, under the laburnum-tree. Here Betty was working hard one morning, when, having finished her lessons with unusual quickness, she was allowed out of the schoolroom half an hour before the others.

A more unpromising site for a garden it would have been difficult to imagine. All that the ordinary world saw were two stone slabs, that had something to do with lighting a cellar below the house. But the children had long ago discovered, that one stone being several inches higher than the other, water poured on it would rush like a miniature cascade to the lower level. This was by no means the only possibility of amusement that the stones afforded. A large crack ran down the centre of each, and these when properly blocked with mud at either end made two admirable lakes. There were other smaller cracks, in which the children from time to time planted a daisy or a laburnum seed. Once or twice they had been known to grow, which was distinctly encouraging.

This little pleasure-ground had lately suffered considerable neglect, owing to the number of exciting events that had occurred. Besides, when Madge was out of doors she liked larger and more energetic amusements. But Betty was devoted to arranging her little garden in new ways, and directly she found herself alone she began to work out a scheme for beautifying it that she had long had in her head. The lakes were carefully formed with some nice sticky handfuls of clay at either end to keep in the water. This had often been done before, but it was quite a new thing, and entirely Betty's own idea, to cover the mud banks with glittering fragments of gravel, so that they looked like rockeries. She also stuck bits of grass round the edges to do duty for rushes, and very well they looked. But the most happy thought of all was making imitation water-lilies out of nasturtium leaves. When that was done, Betty stopped to admire her work with very natural pride. It seemed almost as perfect as human skill could make it.

At that moment up came John. He had finished his lessons before Madge, who, it seemed, had got into difficulties over her sums, from which she was not likely to emerge until dinner-time. John admired the new arrangements exceedingly, and also contributed a suggestion to the effect that there should be a fleet on the lake.

"Yes, but one of our boats will fill up the whole lake," said Betty, who did not quite appreciate having her own arrangements interfered with by a new-comer.

John made no direct answer, but dipping his hand deep into his pocket, he drew out about a dozen nut-shells and deposited them on the stone.

Betty examined the heap carefully. "There isn't a single kernel left, not half a one!" she said in a tone of disappointment. "What's the good of bringing those?"

"Boats, don't you see?" explained John. And really the nut-shells, such of them at least as were not too utterly smashed, made excellent boats, in exact proportion to the size of the lake. When a little extra excitement was required, Betty scraped away the mud that blocked back the water on the upper stone, and a cataract rushed out, bearing the whole fleet with it, and plunged recklessly into the depths of the lower pool.

Once they adjourned for a short time to another little garden that had lately been planned out in the middle of a shrubbery. To approach it, one had first to cross a broad flower-border that edged the shrubbery. Theoretically the children always jumped this flower-bed, leaving no trace of their footsteps, but in practice, as it was rather wide, they usually alighted heavily in the middle of it. Many a broken geranium and crushed heliotrope testified to their unsuccessful efforts, and Captain West, having no clue to their proceedings, was often driven to wonder what charm—except naughtiness—there could be about jumping on the flower-beds. He had not penetrated into the middle of the shrubbery for years; never since the laurels and hollies had grown into a solid prickly barrier against the outer world. So he could not possibly guess that somewhere out of sight a weakly bush had been gradually choked to death by its more robust companions, and that the children on one of their voyages of discovery had noticed this, and decided that since the poor thing was nearly dead it would obviously be more sensible to pull it up and make a garden in its place. Of course, the ground was so full of the roots of trees that ordinary digging was quite out of the question; a spade (even if Madge stepped on it with both feet and all her weight) would not go in more than half an inch. But in the end the children very satisfactorily scratched up the ground for about a square yard with pointed sticks, and put in a row of primroses upside down, because they had been told that if planted in that position they would come up red. This experiment failed with the greatest regularity year after year in whatever corner of the garden it was tried. Yet both children and gardeners are such hopeful people, that when the two are combined one may expect to see absolutely impossible feats cheerfully embarked upon as often as the sun rises.

Betty and John did not go to this charming retreat empty-handed. The former had some plants torn up by the roots, the latter a half-filled watering-pot. The fact was that several small things had been left over after finishing the naval display, and it seemed a pity to waste them. Water, for instance, was always valuable, because there was a certain amount of difficulty about getting it. The gardener objected to their drawing off much from his pump, which was apt to run dry in hot weather, while if they went indoors to get a drop from a tap they were at once set upon by innumerable people ordering them not to make messes and wet their frocks. So when some water was left over from flooding the lake, it was proposed not to throw it away, but to carry it to the shrubbery garden, where there were several languishing plants. There was the inevitable little struggle for possession of the watering-pot; but Betty was not unreasonable, so she gave it up when John pointed out that she had the undivided enjoyment of it while he was at lessons. And in its place she carried two or three very drooping nasturtium plants, that had unfortunately come up by the roots while she was picking their leaves. They would do very well to plant in the shrubbery, where the sun could never manage to pierce the screen of overhanging boughs even at mid-day. All gardeners know that a hot sun has a very disastrous effect on newly-moved plants, especially if their roots are mostly torn off.

"I'll hold the watering-pot while you jump over the geranium-bed," said Betty. "You know we broke two last week, and Papa said if he caught—"

"Nonsense! It's only you girls with your skirts who break things," interrupted John, clutching his watering-pot tighter than ever, for he strongly suspected his sister of intending to wile it away from him. He jumped, the watering-pot was heavy, and the weight all on one side. Consequently he fell, and his fall was unusually disastrous, being marked by more than the ordinary number of crushed geraniums and scattered earth. Of course the water was all upset, principally into his boots: and Betty threw away her nasturtiums in disgust, for it was quite useless to plant them dry, and they had both been warned off the pump and the tap that very morning. There might easily have been some rather bitter reproaches at this point, but fortunately Madge was sent out to summon them to dinner.

"I want you to do something for me this afternoon," she said to Betty and John as they returned to the house. "Miss Thompson is going to take me to Churchbury shopping, and I think Lewis will be expecting me at the Eagle's Nest. I said something about it yesterday before I knew that I was going shopping."

"But why can't John and I go and talk to him?" answered Betty. "We aren't all going shopping."

"You don't think he will care to talk to little things like you?" laughed Madge. "Why, he is two years older than me even; but, of course, that isn't much. I only want you to tell him why I haven't come, and that we shall have the usual afternoon holiday on Saturday. Then you can come straight back, for I am sure he won't stop with you."

Since the day that Jack jumped over the wall Lewis had talked to the children several times, standing close under the tree, and keeping an anxious eye in the direction of Mrs. Howard's house all the while. Of course he could not climb up to play with them since the rope-ladder so mysteriously disappeared. There had been no explanation of that strange disappearance. At first the children feared that Barton had found their hiding-place, and recovered his missing property; but they soon made up their minds that this could not be the case, when the old man continued to meet them every day without any signs of anger. For when Barton suspected that they had been in mischief, he did not hesitate to scold them severely himself, and also complain to their father. They often got into trouble this way when he found them hunting the pigs too vigorously, or playing tricks with the milk-pails. He would certainly have made a great fuss about their borrowing his ropes without leave, and knotting them all over. So, as he said nothing, it was pretty certain that he knew nothing.

But though Lewis Brand was now completely cut off from the Eagle's Nest, being on a lower level by about a dozen feet than the children who were sitting in it, he contrived to tell them a wonderful number of stories about himself and the bad treatment which he suffered, speaking all the while in a loud whisper that was very impressive. In this way they heard, among other curious facts, that the gray-bearded man was the jailer of whose cruelties Lewis had already told them. The children were surprised at this, for the gray-bearded man had not looked either very powerful or very savage. But they accepted from Lewis the explanation that he was a hypocrite.

CHAPTER XII
A NEW LADDER

John and Betty started rather unwillingly on their task. It seemed sadly dull to walk across several fields under a burning sun merely to deliver a message for Madge, while she was enjoying an afternoon among the Churchbury shops. Of course they were at perfect liberty to stay playing in the Eagle's Nest as long as they liked. But somehow they did not care to linger there by themselves. Without Madge's substantial protection the shade of the spreading beech-trees seemed more gloomy, and the distance from the house greater, even than usual. Besides, when Madge was not present to remind them of the laws of trespass, they could not help feeling as if Mrs. Howard might pounce upon them at any moment and drag them over the wall to her darkest cellars. So they only intended just to give their message to Lewis if he appeared, and then to hurry back to those little gardens of which they were so fond, where there was always something to be done, and no fear of being kidnapped.

However, everything turned out as differently as possible to what they had expected. No sooner had they climbed on to the Eagle's Nest than they heard a low whistle, and looking down saw Lewis gliding along on his side of the wall with the stealthy tread of an Indian on an enemy's trail. He was a thin boy, with a white face, and always looked over his shoulder as if he expected some foe to be coming up behind him.

"Madge can't come. She had to go to Churchbury shopping. She told us to tell you," said Betty, leaning down from her perch and speaking as low as she could. The children at Beechgrove shouted so much when they were at home, that it was always a great effort to them to lower their voices. Lewis, on the contrary, had the art of carrying on a long conversation all in whispers, it seemed natural to him.

"All right! Never mind. We can do just as well without her," was the unexpected answer.

Betty looked puzzled. "Shall I give her any message from you about Saturday?" Betty said, preparing to leave the Eagle's Nest.

"What are you in such a hurry to be off for?" cried Lewis, rather louder than usual. "Aren't you going to stop and talk?"

"But Madge isn't here, and—"

"Oh, bother Madge!" interrupted Lewis. "You and John aren't her slaves, are you? Can't we have a bit of fun by ourselves for once, without having her interfering and trying to manage everything? I often wonder you two stand it! I know I wouldn't!"

"But I thought you and Madge were such friends!" said Betty, much bewildered by the strangeness of this declaration.

"She thinks you don't care to speak to us. Only to her, because she is older," chimed in John.

"Well, that's just where she makes a mistake," said Lewis roughly. "I can't abide girls who think they are so grand, and are always ordering other people about! Why, to hear her talk of this Eagle's Nest one would believe she made it all herself, and I daresay you and John worked just as hard as she did."

Now until this moment it had never struck Betty and John as strange that Madge should take the lead in everything. She was the oldest, biggest, and strongest of the three; and if she usually had her own way about everything, it had only seemed natural to the others that this should be so. Besides, she took all the trouble of making plans for them, and they really had much more fun under her guidance than they would have had alone. So it was quite a new view to them that they were oppressed, but when it had once been put into their heads they began to think that perhaps they had something to complain of after all.

"Now you won't be such silly sneaks as to go and tell Madge everything I have been saying?" observed Lewis rather anxiously when he noticed what a serious impression his words were making. "If you are such babies as that I shall never speak to you again. And I have not been saying any harm either, you know." He was beginning to fear, from the twins' solemn faces, that they would go home and repeat his words to Madge. "Only I have always thought you two looked such jolly little things, if your sister would give you a chance of being spoken to, or played with," he added.

All this was excessively flattering coming from a big boy of fourteen, and after some more remarks of the sort Betty and John began to feel that they were very fine people, who had always, rather unjustly, been kept in the background by their elder sister. For the first time in their lives they looked upon Madge as a tyrant.

"I should like to come up there and play with you," continued Lewis. "Only the wall is rather too high for me to climb now that the ladder has gone. Oh, I have a good idea! Capital! The very thing! Why didn't we think of it before, I wonder?"

"What is it?" cried the twins. "What have you thought of?"

Lewis did not answer, but turned away and ran quickly to the shed where Jack had been shut up. Presently he came out again, dragging some iron railings, which with considerable trouble he got as far as the overhanging boughs of the beech-tree.

"There's a ladder for you!" he exclaimed proudly, as he propped the railings against the wall.

"It's splendid! Quite splendid!" shouted the twins, forgetting in their excitement how near they were to the terrible house with the cellar.

"Hush! Hush!" whispered Lewis. "If you make such a noise we shall be caught, and all our fun stopped. And it's not quite perfect either. Not high enough. See!"

In point of fact the top bar of the railings was only five feet from the ground, so that it did not reach more than half-way up the wall. It was very nice as far as it went, but more of it was badly wanted. However, Lewis was not easily discouraged. He returned to the shed, where there were several more railings, and dragged out another. "They are dreadfully heavy," he said; "but I don't care. I shall go on fetching them until I get enough to reach the top of the wall. I know there are a heap of them in the shed. They are kept there when they are not being used to divide the field."

"Take care you don't tumble! Oh, that's beautiful! I do wish we could help you!" cried the twins, looking on in the highest admiration while Lewis slowly pushed and pulled one railing on the top of another against the wall. Then he tied them together with some bits of string out of his pocket, and proceeded to mount. It was not a very steady ladder, but with the wall to lean against there was small fear of falling, and when near the top of it Lewis could reach the hands that were eagerly stretched out to help him. In another moment he was sitting on the Eagle's Nest.

"This is a goodish sort of tree," he remarked, looking round with a patronizing air. "Very easy to climb, of course—"

"Oh, but I can go much higher than these boughs by the wall!" interrupted Betty. "So high that my feet are where your head is now."

"That's not much," said Lewis scornfully. "Girls never can climb much. They just flop about, and catch their frocks in all the branches, and get giddy, and cry to be helped down again!"

The Eagle's Nest | 61

Betty flushed hotly. "You are talking nonsense!" she shrieked. "Silly nonsense! I can climb much higher than John; and as for crying—"

Her remarks were promptly cut short by a hand being roughly pressed over her mouth. "Hold your tongue!" whispered Lewis. "Unless you wish old Mother Howard and her slave-drivers to be after us!"

At this terrible threat Betty looked nervously towards the brick house. But there was nothing to be seen in that direction except the quiet old cows in the orchard below. She was so reassured by seeing them chewing the cud, as if nothing dreadful could possibly happen, that she regained sufficient courage to remark defiantly that after all Mrs. Howard did not seem a very formidable person.

"That shows all you know about it!" replied Lewis. "I can tell you a very different tale. If you two will promise faithfully not to say a single word of what I tell you to anybody—not to Madge, or your nurse, or anybody,—then I will tell you something that nobody else knows. Only it's a secret, you must remember,—a dead secret."

This was very solemn work. Betty and John glanced at each other, both longing to know the secret, and yet a little afraid of the conditions that had been imposed.

"Mightn't we just tell Madge if she promises not to repeat it?" Betty ventured to say.

"Certainly not! We don't want Madge poking her interfering nose into everything, do we?" replied Lewis rudely. "Just make up your minds whether you want to hear a most terrible and extraordinary thing, or not, for I can't wait much longer. But if I don't tell you to-day I sha'n't breathe a word of it another time, so it's no good teasing me again."

This last remark decided Betty. She was very curious by nature, and could not bear to miss any piece of news that promised to be interesting.

"I think I must hear the secret, although I would much rather tell Madge about it," she said in a hesitating voice. "And if you don't like to promise, John, you must go a little way off and stop your ears."

But John was not equal to so much self-restraint. If Betty had resisted the temptation of hearing the secret he would have done so too, but he could not possibly let her enjoy the advantage of knowing more than he did. "I promise not to tell," he grunted.

"Ah, that's all very well!" exclaimed Lewis; "but I must see if you two babies can keep a secret. Just put out your hands. Now I am going to pinch your little fingers, and if you cry out it means that you can't be trusted." And pinch he did, and very hard too, but the twins bravely clenched their teeth and said nothing.

When Lewis had teased them to his heart's content, he began his wonderful tale by whispering in a mysterious voice:

"Do you know what Mrs. Howard really is?"

"An old lady," replied Betty very naturally. "Your aunt, perhaps? No? But she looks rather like it, doesn't she?"

"Ah! but she is something quite different really," said Lewis. And after pausing a short time to heighten Betty's curiosity, he added: "She is a witch!"

The twins started back, hardly able to believe their ears. "But there aren't any witches now!" they cried. "Besides, there aren't such things really. They used to be burned, but Miss Thompson says most likely they were only poor old women who couldn't hurt anybody."

"I don't care a bit what Miss Thompson or anybody says," replied Lewis. "Mrs. Howard is an old witch, you can tell that by the black cat that follows her everywhere. That's a sure sign."

Betty hardly knew what to say, for she had once seen a picture of a witch, and there was undoubtedly a black cat crouching in the corner of it.

"You noticed the way she shook her head, I dare say?" continued Lewis, who was delighted by the awestruck looks of his two companions. "Well, she is muttering spells when she does that. She has the power to destroy things if she says the right words. Any morning I may wake up and find the house changed into a heap of dust, or perhaps be struck dead myself."

It seemed impossible that such things should be going on almost within sight of Miss Thompson's schoolroom window. And yet, judging by the gravity of Lewis's face, he was speaking in most sober earnest. John and Betty pressed tighter together, and took hold of each other's hands.

"I hope for your sakes that the old witch won't find out you've been talking to me," continued Lewis solemnly.

"Why what would she do?" Betty ventured to ask.

"That would depend on what sort of a temper she happened to be in," was the reassuring reply.

And then Lewis proceeded to tell such terrible tales about Mrs. Howard's power and malignity, that the poor twins longed to be safely back at home, out of sight of that weird brick house, whose commonplace walls concealed such dreadful deeds of cruelty.

CHAPTER XIII
THE BROWN BAG

Madge was spending her afternoon in a still more stirring manner than the twins. A shopping expedition to Churchbury was always an excitement, and it was extraordinary how many little purchases seemed absolutely necessary directly the children found out that one of them was going to town.

Madge was heavily laden with money. Five shillings and sevenpence, mostly in coppers, take up a great deal of room. This sum represented the joint property of Madge, Betty, and John. They collected it in a tin money-box shaped like a small doll's house, with a slit in the roof to drop in the pennies. Miss Thompson kept the key of the front-door, and they had to apply to her for it before any money could be taken out. They had made this rule themselves, because they found that unless their money was locked up so that they could not get at it without a little trouble, they used it as soon as it was given them. To-day they had all three asked for the key, and opened the front-door with pleasant anticipations of finding a fortune inside. They were able to judge in some measure of the probable extent of their fortune by the weight of the tin house. Luckily there was no space required for sitting-rooms or stairs inside the house (which was in fact rather a sham, being really nothing better than a box), so that it would hold an almost unlimited quantity of money. Even five shillings and sevenpence did not half fill it.

Of course Madge could not take a tin house with chimneys in her pocket to Churchbury on a shopping expedition, and she signally failed in an attempt to squeeze the money into her purse. Betty and John offered theirs in addition; but at this point she was met by a fresh difficulty, no pocket will hold three purses unnaturally distended with pennies.

"I really do think I had better only take my share and leave you two your own money to spend another day," Madge had observed rather dolefully, for she had been looking forward with some pride to the unusually substantial purchases that the possession of their united fortunes would enable her to make.

But John and Betty would not hear of this suggestion for a moment. They were longing to spend their saved-up hoards of money, and as there was no immediate prospect of their going to Churchbury themselves, they had been counting on Madge returning in the evening laden with interesting purchases.

There was a short period of dismayed silence. Then Betty suddenly broke out: "I know a way! Wait just a second!"

She rushed excitedly off, and returned waving a neat bag of shiny brown calico.

"Why, that's what Nurse made for you to pack your best shoes in when you went away on visits!" exclaimed Madge.

"Yes, it was made out of a bit of lining that was left over from Mama's last winter dress, and it has got a wreathing-string and everything," replied Betty proudly. "It really seems as if Nurse had made it on purpose for a money-bag."

To make a long story short, the brown calico bag appeared so exactly suited to hold the sum of five shillings and sevenpence (mostly in pennies), that it would have been a stupid neglect of opportunities not to use it. Madge quickly emptied the contents of the tin house into their new resting-place, and then started for Churchbury with the comfortable feeling of having practically boundless wealth at her disposal.

Now it happened that Miss Thompson had several errands of a peculiarly uninteresting nature to do in the town, as Mrs. West had asked her to buy a number of things for the household. Generally the children enjoyed being inside any sort of shop, but after watching Miss Thompson carefully select dusters and pantry-clothes, cotton, tape, and buttons, for what appeared an interminable time, Madge sighed deeply.

"If you are tired of sitting still you may go outside and look at the shop windows," said Miss Thompson. "I have not nearly finished yet, and it fidgets me to hear you sighing in such a despairing way."

"It's only because I'm afraid of not having time to buy all the things we want if we stay here so long," explained Madge.

"Why, what do you want?"

"Oh, Miss Thompson! You know we have five shillings and sevenpence to spend!" cried Madge reproachfully. "And we all want a nice thing apiece out of it, and one or two little extra things if there is money enough."

"And you have not yet decided on what you are going to buy, I suppose," said Miss Thompson; "and are waiting to choose until you get into the right sort of shop?"

Madge admitted that this was the case.

"But if I may go outside and walk up and down the street, I dare say I shall find something in the windows by the time you are ready," she added.

Miss Thompson thought this rather a good plan, as she knew from past experience what a very long time it always took the children to decide on how to lay out their money to the best advantage. So after Madge had been solemnly warned not to wander far, she was allowed to go out in the street by herself for a few minutes.

It was an exciting moment when the little girl found herself walking sedately up the pavement alone. She had never been quite so independent before in her life, and she hoped that the passers-by all noticed there was not any grown-up person in charge of her. But they were mostly too occupied to take any interest in this event. Possibly there were so many little girls in Churchbury that the appearance of one extra did not strike people as particularly remarkable.

At any rate Madge herself felt all the importance of the occasion. She walked soberly along with the heavy little brown bag hanging from her wrist by its string. Secured in this way, there was no chance of her forgetting its existence and leaving it on the counter of a shop. She had done this once with a purse, and Miss Thompson had been obliged to go back to most of the places where she had been shopping before she could recover it for Madge. But a brown bag tied firmly round the wrist of its owner really seemed safe from any sort of accident.

Madge had no wish to wander far away, but unfortunately the dulness of the large linen-draper's shop that she had just left seemed to pervade its neighbours on either side; for about fifty yards there was nothing to be seen but highly respectable and uninteresting tailors' and shoemakers' establishments. Thus it came about that Madge walked almost to the end of the street before she found a shop window that held any objects of the kind for which she was looking. At last she stopped in front of a small stationer's. There, arranged among the piles of writing-paper and envelopes, were a quantity of little ornaments and toys.

Madge was growing rather old to care about regular playthings, and yet she could not resist the charms of a tiny doll's dressing-table covered with miniature hair-brushes and combs. She wondered how much it cost, and whether Betty would want to share it with her.

"John won't care for it, I suppose," she muttered to herself. "At least he will think it grander to pretend that he doesn't like such a girlish thing, though I dare say he will always be wanting to play with it. After all, one can't choose things that will suit everybody, and I know I could make such a dear little pin-cushion to stand on that table, with very small pins stuck into it in a pattern. I've got a bit of silk that would do exactly—Oh! What has happened? Oh, dear! oh, dear!"

Poor Madge! While thinking over the various ways in which she could amuse herself with the doll's dressing-table, she had been excitedly swinging the little brown bag up and down by the string. Five shillings and sevenpence, mostly in pennies, is rather heavy; an insecurely tied knot gave way, and the bag suddenly fell with a loud clatter—not to the ground, that would have been a very bearable misfortune, but through a grating in the pavement on which Madge happened to be standing at the moment.

It does not often fall to a person's lot to drop his whole fortune down a grating into someone else's cellar. It seemed to Madge as if no such terrible fate had ever overtaken a human being before. If the brown bag had contained nothing but her own money, she would have preferred leaving it where it fell, to making a fuss about recovering it. She could not bear to be thought stupid, and yet it did not seem very clever to have lost the bag of which she was professing to take so much care. But as Betty's and John's money had also disappeared down the dark grating, it seemed quite hopeless to hush the matter up. They would naturally question her until they found out the truth, and then loudly express their opinion of her selfishness if she had not made every possible effort to recover their missing property.

Madge looked despairingly down the street in the hope of seeing Miss Thompson, but only an unceasing stream of strangers passed and repassed the spot where she stood. Then she stooped down and peered through the grating. It was so dark down below that she could not distinguish the bag; only, of course, having seen it fall, and even heard the clatter of some of the coins as they rolled out, she knew it must be there. She did not like to leave the spot and go back to Miss Thompson. It seemed as if the money would be more likely to disappear in her absence; although she could not really take care of it by standing on top of the grating, yet she felt as if she could.

While hesitating what to do next, Madge happened to look through the window of the stationer's shop, and saw an elderly woman sitting behind the counter. She had spectacles on her nose, and such a very mild appearance that Madge at last decided to go in and explain the whole matter to her. If the woman would only let her run down to the cellar and pick up the money, nobody at home need ever know anything about the silly accident.

CHAPTER XIV
KEEPING SHOP

"Please may I just look in your cellar for a minute?" began Madge very politely, as she entered the shop. "I am very sorry to trouble you, but I won't be long."

"What did you say you wanted, miss?" inquired the old woman, thinking that she had not heard correctly what Madge asked for. "You must excuse me, miss," she went on, "for ever since I had the influenza last winter my hearing has not been what it was before. It's very awkward in the shop, as you may think. Many days I get one of my grand-children, a little girl about your age, to come and help me, but this week she has gone off to visit an aunt in London. Of course that was a great treat for her, so I couldn't think of interfering with it, and I am trying to do the best I can alone."

Another time Madge would have been much interested in hearing all about the little girl who helped her grandmother to keep shop; but now she was in a great hurry to get her money back before Miss Thompson came to look for her, so directly the old woman stopped speaking she began a more detailed explanation of what she wanted, in a particularly clear voice.

"If it was only my own money I wouldn't interrupt you to look for it," she said, "although it is five shillings and sevenpence. But it belongs to the others as well, and, of course, they are expecting me to choose all sorts of nice things in the shops. They will be so disappointed if I don't get it back in time to buy something before we have to start home. It seemed so safe in a brown money-bag, you know; at least it was really Betty's shoe-bag, only she took them out and put them in her drawer. I don't think Nurse knew she had done it. But what I wanted to tell you was, that I believe I can find it in a minute if you will only let me run down to your cellar."

It is to be feared that the old woman understood even less than she heard of this long speech. One sentence, however, reached her ears, and to this she replied.

"I haven't any cellar, miss," she said.

"But—but—" Madge did not dare contradict her flatly. Yet there was the grating in the pavement outside. "Please come to the door a minute," she cried, "and I will show you what I mean, Mrs— Oh, I am so sorry! I don't know your name!"

"My name is Mrs. Winter, and I've kept this shop ever since I became a widow thirty years ago," said the old woman. Then pitying Madge's blushes she continued: "It doesn't matter about not knowing my name, miss. Don't give it another thought. Mrs. Winter is my name, as I said, and it is certainly written above the door, but perhaps you didn't notice it."

"No, I didn't look there! That was very stupid indeed of me!" exclaimed Madge, who had been rather afraid that the old woman might be vexed at her name not being better known. "But I shall remember that you are Mrs. Winter always now," she added. "And now please let me show you where the brown bag dropped."

"Ah, down there was it?" said Mrs. Winter, coming to the door. "You will have a troublesome job to get in there, I am afraid. That cellar belongs to the large house next door that's empty. The whole place is shut up, and the man who keeps the key lives at the other side of the town."

"What shall I do? What shall I do?" repeated poor Madge, her spirits quite giving way at this discouraging news. Up to that time she had fancied that if she could once explain the state of the case to Mrs. Winter all would be well. And now it turned out that after all Mrs. Winter had no more power to get back the bag than Madge herself. Of course at twelve years old one can't cry before strangers, but if Madge had only been the same age as the twins, it is very certain that she would have relieved herself by bursting into tears. Even as it was she looked so miserable as to excite Mrs. Winter's compassion.

"There! Don't you fret about your money, my dear," she said, patting Madge kindly on the shoulder. "It will be all safe down that grating, never fear! There are too many locked doors to the house for anybody to run away with it, and the rats and spiders won't do it any harm. And when the man who keeps the key comes to open the windows and air the rooms a bit I'll try and catch him. He is generally here about once or twice a week, and I'll see that you get back your money safe enough."

"It's very kind of you," said Madge dolefully; "but I am afraid it will not be of much use unless I can get back the money this afternoon. You see, we live in the country, and we hardly ever come to Churchbury; only now and then for a great treat. And Betty and John are expecting their toys this evening, or books, or chocolates. I was to choose whatever I thought they would like best, and now I can't get anything."

"Dear! dear!" exclaimed kind Mrs. Winter, in a tone of deep concern. And then she proceeded to ask a great many questions about what had happened.

As Madge finished her sad story the old woman broke out into lamentations.

"If only I had someone to keep the shop for half an hour I would go after the man myself and try to get the key, that I would," she said. "But little Ann is away, and—"

"Who is little Ann?" interrupted Madge.

"Why, my grandchild to be sure!" rejoined Mrs. Winter. "And not so little either, only that's a manner of speaking I got into when she was a baby, and now I keep on forgetting that she has turned thirteen and able to help me in the shop as well as any grown-up woman."

"I shall be thirteen very soon myself," said Madge eagerly. "Don't you think I could stay in the shop just as Ann does, while you go to find the man with the key? Oh, please let me try! I'm sure I could manage it if you are quick."

Mrs. Winter hesitated. It is true that Madge was just as tall as her own grand-daughter, but then Ann knew the ways of the shop; and it was a very different thing leaving her in charge to confiding all one's property to the care of a perfect stranger. Mrs. Winter, however, did not feel any distrust of Madge, and quite believed the story about the lost bag of money. She could see that it was not the invention of an impostor, who wished to get an opportunity for pilfering little things out of the shop. In fact, the more Mrs. Winter thought about the case the more inclined she felt to help in the recovery of the brown bag. She was one if those kindly people who naturally interest themselves in their neighbours' affairs, and she felt strongly tempted to take a part in the little adventure.

"After all it's no great work to stand behind the counter and see that the things are safe," said Mrs. Winter reflectively.

"Oh, yes, I'm sure I could do that!" replied Madge. "But then if anybody came to buy. They do sometimes, I suppose?"

"Of course they do, or what would be the sense of calling it a shop," said Mrs. Winter rather sharply. "You mustn't think because you caught me just sitting down to knit for a few minutes this afternoon that business is in any way slack. That's just my quiet time for an hour or so then. But you wait till about tea-time, and there isn't standing room for anyone in the shop many an evening. I know I could do with another pair of hands easily! What with one wanting writing-paper, and another pencils, and another a bottle of ink, it may be! And the children running in with their pennies to ask for some of the little things you may have noticed in the window; I always keep a lot of knick-knacks for them."

All this sounded very alarming. Even Madge began to doubt her own capacity for standing behind the counter and awaiting such an overpowering rush of business. However, she presently remembered that Mrs. Winter had referred to the afternoon as being usually a very quiet time, and certainly nothing could have looked more peaceful than the old woman sitting quietly nodding over her knitting, and occasionally flicking a speck of dust off the goods nearest her. Besides, on careful consideration, the shop was so small that three or four customers would have great difficulty in getting inside it at once, so perhaps the crowd of which Mrs. Winter spoke was not really of such an alarming size. At all events she wanted to get the brown bag back very much, and it was worth risking something for its recovery.

After a great deal of persuasion Mrs. Winter consented to put on her bonnet and go in search of the man with the key. Up to the last moment she poured out an unceasing flow of instructions to Madge how to behave under every possible circumstance. "And if anybody should come while I am away, which it's to be hoped they won't, you must just make a bit of conversation about the weather or something till I come back," she concluded. "That's what Ann does when I've stepped out for a moment, and she doesn't know the price of a thing somebody inquires for. Why, the child will chat away as cleverly as possible about the new electric lights in the town, or the spring flower-show, or what not, and nobody could ever guess that she is only filling up the time till I come back! And that's what you must try and do." With these words Mrs. Winter left the shop.

It was a funny position for Madge, left all alone in charge of a shop. If anybody had told her that it was going to happen she would have been delighted at such an amusing prospect, and would certainly not have been troubled by any modest doubts as to her power of selling like a regular shop-woman. But now that the situation had actually come to pass she felt unusually nervous, and very much hoped that her talents would not be tested by any customer coming while she was alone. For the first quarter of an hour she stood anxiously staring through the glass at the passers-by, expecting each person to stop and come in at the door. Nobody came, however, and in spite of Mrs. Winter's repeated assurances of the popularity of her little shop, it seemed strangely neglected that afternoon by the inhabitants of Churchbury.

Madge gradually became calmer as she found that nothing was going to happen, and with the comfortable reflection that Mrs. Winter must be back before long she began to amuse herself by examining the contents of the shop.

CHAPTER XV
A CUSTOMER

It was really very interesting to be inside the counter instead of outside, and in a position to examine everything carefully without any interference. On the rare occasions when Madge, Betty, and John went shopping, it always seemed to them as if no sooner had they caught a glimpse of some especially fascinating book, picture, or toy, than they were instantly hauled away to one of those dull linen-draper's establishments in which grown-up people so mysteriously delight to linger. As for examining anything closely, that was quite out of the question when they went shopping with Miss Thompson. Ever since the time when Betty had knocked two china ornaments off a shelf and broken them to pieces while stretching out her hand to pick up a pepper-pot in the shape of an owl, there had been a strict rule that the children should touch nothing in shops. It was a dreadfully dull rule, because, of course, nobody can look at things comfortably from a yard off and without handling them at all. The prettiest doll loses most of its interest if one cannot count how many petticoats there are under its dress, and examine how much of its neck is made of wax, and where the stuffing begins. And what can be duller than a mechanical mouse, unless one can wind it up to run on the floor?

Madge decided at once that under such very peculiar circumstances as the present she need not keep to Miss Thompson's rule. After all it would be simply ridiculous to be standing inside the counter and left in charge of the shop without even daring to look at the things she was supposed to be selling. So, to provide herself as it were with a good excuse, she took up a duster that she found lying on a chair, and began carefully to rub over all the interesting things. The piles of envelopes and writing-paper Madge did not consider required much dusting, but pen-wipers in the shape of pigs, and work-boxes covered with shells arranged in patterns, clearly called for a great deal of attention.

Although Mrs. Winter was very particular about calling her shop a stationer's, she really seemed to sell a little of everything. Madge could see very well that it was just the kind of place where she would be able to choose the sort of interesting things that Betty and John expected. When she got her money back she would set seriously to work to spend it at Mrs. Winter's before she met with any further misadventures.

"It isn't many people who have first kept a shop and then bought things out of it all in one afternoon, I should think," she said aloud, as she vigorously dusted a mug adorned with coloured portraits of the royal family.

At that moment there was a great push, and the door flew open.

"How quick you have been!" began Madge; then she stopped suddenly and almost dropped the mug. It was not Mrs. Winter who came in, but a girl a few years older than herself, evidently a customer.

"I want a fashion-paper," said the new-comer in a harsh voice. "One of those with big coloured pictures of ladies in party-dresses and ball-gowns. Something smart, you know. It's for myself—Miss Amelia Block of Ivy Villa."

Madge felt that she was expected to know the name, and that Miss Amelia Block was, in her own estimation at least, a very important person. Perhaps she was in the habit of buying fashion-papers at this shop. She probably had copied her hat, which was very large and profusely trimmed with pink ribbon, out of one of the coloured pictures of which she seemed so fond. It was a pity, Madge thought, that her face, instead of being pretty and smiling, as the ladies are always represented in fashion-papers, was ugly and cross-looking. And a pair of very dirty gray kid gloves, with most of their buttons off, did not improve her appearance by any means.

"I do hope she intends to buy some new gloves before she has any more smart dresses or hats made," Madge could not help thinking.

In the meantime Miss Block was walking slowly round, or to speak more correctly, turning on her heels, in the middle of the tiny shop. "You don't seem to have much choice of fashion-papers here," she said rudely.

Madge did not reply, for the very excellent reason that she had not an idea what fashion-papers Mrs. Winter kept.

"Haven't you anything more stylish than this?" inquired Miss Block, picking up an illustrated magazine off the counter, and pointing contemptuously to the picture of two ladies in their best dresses on the cover. "I'm going to several parties and bazaars," she explained, "and, of course, I don't want to look a regular dowdy."

"No, I see you don't," said Madge, staring at the enormous pink hat, and then without intending it her eyes suddenly fell to the dirty gray kid gloves.

Miss Block evidently thought that the little girl was intentionally trying to make her feel uncomfortable. She became very red, and hurriedly hid her hands in the folds of her skirt.

"If you will kindly give me what I asked for at once, instead of standing there giggling at your betters, I'll be very much obliged to you," she said, speaking even more disagreeably than before.

Madge was quite taken aback by this address. She never had the least intention of behaving rudely, although it was true that in the bottom of her heart she did not at all admire Miss Block's appearance. Still, she had not meant to show her feelings so plainly. While she stood speechless, wondering how she could best beg her customer's pardon, Miss Block burst out into a storm of abuse that would better have befitted a neglected street child than such a very smartly dressed young woman.

"You just wait a bit till I see your grandmother!" she cried. "I'll soon give her a bit of my mind for leaving such a vulgar chit of a child in charge of her shop! It's my own fault I suppose for coming to such a low place instead of going to the largest shops in the town, which I might as well do. And in future I shall certainly go where I shall be treated like a young lady! Mrs. Winter needn't look for my patronage any more, I can tell you. She may think I am going to submit quietly to being insulted by her pert little granddaughter, but she will soon find out—"

"Please, I am not Mrs. Winter's grandchild, so you need not say that!" interrupted Madge, suddenly recovering the use of her voice. Her anger at this undeserved abuse almost got the better of her shyness. "I've got nothing to do with Mrs. Winter," she continued. "But it's a nice shop and I won't hear it abused. I dare say there are heaps of fashion-papers in it, only I don't know where to find them—"

"If you aren't Mrs. Winter's grand-daughter, who are you then, I should very much like to know?" said Miss Block, looking at Madge curiously across the counter.

"That's no business of yours," replied Madge, with more truth than politeness. In point of fact she did not wish this very disagreeable young person to find out her name. It seemed as if the adventure might end rather sillily, and Madge was not at all anxious for her part in it to be widely known.

Miss Block did not appear daunted by the abrupt answer she had received. On the contrary, she gave a curious smile when Madge declined to tell her name, and nodded her head, repeating softly to herself, "I thought so. Just as I thought."

"What did you think?" said Madge at last, feeling intolerably irritated at her customer's mysterious words and manners.

"Well, it wouldn't require a very clever person to guess what you are!" replied Miss Block triumphantly. She spoke as if she had just made some great discovery that gave her infinite pleasure.

"You don't really know who I am, do you?" said Madge with considerable anxiety.

"Well, I am generally considered as sharp as my neighbours, I believe!" retorted Miss Block. "And I can make a pretty good guess! When I find somebody in a shop who doesn't know where any of the things are kept, although I see her pulling them all about as I come in; and when she gets very frightened, and won't tell her name or how she got there, I call that person a thief!"

"A thief! You think I am a thief!" cried Madge, almost more astonished than offended by such an extraordinary accusation. "Why, Mrs. Winter herself told me to stay in the shop while she went off to find the man who—"

"Oh yes! A very fine story. I have heard of that kind of excuse before!" interrupted Miss Block mockingly. "It's my belief you just slipped in when poor old Mrs. Winter was out of the way for a minute, and if I hadn't luckily caught you in the very act you would have been off with your pockets crammed—"

"How can you say such things!" cried Madge. "Why, I have money to pay for everything I want, only it's dropped down the grating into the cellar of the next house, as I was just going to tell you. And while Mrs. Winter went to get the key I was making up my mind what I would buy presently. And as I have five shillings and sevenpence to spend (it's not all mine exactly, but nearly the same thing), you certainly need not say that I wasn't going to pay!"

"Now that's a very interesting story! So interesting that I'll give you the chance of repeating it to a policeman, and we'll see what he says to it," remarked Miss Block, at the same time moving towards the street door as if to go out.

Madge could hardly believe her ears. A policeman being called to examine her just as if she were really a thief! It seemed impossible, but Miss Block, with a most unpleasant smile, was actually turning the door-handle, when she was suddenly seized round the waist by two strong arms.

"You sha'n't do it!" cried Madge hysterically. "You sha'n't do it, I tell you!"

She was a tall, strong girl for her age, and having sprung on Miss Block from behind and taken her quite by surprise, she had no difficulty in dragging her across the little shop.

Miss Block uttered a series of frightened shrieks and tried to wrench herself free, but though taller she was not nearly so active as Madge. While struggling together the two girls pushed heavily against a door at the back of the shop that led into Mrs. Winter's little sitting-room. It burst open, and they both fell headlong on to a black horse-hair sofa which occupied a prominent position in the room. Madge recovered first from the shock of the fall, and darting back into the shop slammed the door behind her, turning the key in the lock.

CHAPTER XVI
IMPRISONED IN A PARLOUR

On finding herself imprisoned in the little parlour Miss Block began to scream. The noise she had been making before was nothing compared to what she made now. One would never have supposed that the wearer of such a magnificent pink hat could scream as loud as she did. Madge looked anxiously at the faces of the passers-by in the street, but apparently the sounds were considerably softened by coming through two closed doors, at all events nobody took any notice of the turmoil. If only no more customers came to the shop all might be well; but Madge could not help feeling that she was running a great risk of getting mixed up in a really serious affair. Without knowing much about the law, she understood very well that it was exceedingly unusual conduct, to say the least of it, first to knock a strange lady down, and then shut her into somebody else's back parlour. Of course, Madge had rolled over at the same time as her prisoner, and indeed hurt her own elbow rather severely against the wooden framework of the sofa, so that the two girls had really fared very equally. In spite of this Madge felt convinced that Miss Block would describe herself in the future as having been violently assaulted. It might even turn out that, quite unintentionally, Madge had broken the law, and now deserved to be seized by the policeman with whom Miss Block had threatened her a few minutes previously. Then, the very idea of being a fit object for the attention of a policeman seemed absurd; but now Madge could not feel quite as consciously innocent as she would have wished.

Until to-day it had never occurred to Madge that she could possibly break the law except by trespassing on her neighbours' property. The children were all terribly afraid of being caught doing that, because old Barton had often told them warning stories of boys who had been sent to prison for this offence. But now it seemed that it was much easier to get into the clutches of the law than they had imagined. Miss Block between her shrieks might be heard loudly requesting the presence of a policeman, and it could hardly be expected that she would go on much longer without attracting any attention.

On the whole, Madge's best chance of safety seemed to be in trying to make friends with her late adversary. She stood close to the parlour door, and seizing an opportunity when Miss Block's shrieks became a little fainter (probably owing to loss of breath), she put her mouth close to the key-hole and shouted:

"I am very sorry I was rough. Please listen, I have something to say."

Miss Block did not answer, but she did what was still better, she stopped screaming for a minute.

"It was like this," continued Madge, still shouting through the key-hole. "I dropped all our money, five shillings and sevenpence, you know, down the grating in the pavement outside. And when I came and told Mrs. Winter, she promised to fetch the man who kept the key of the house if I would stay—"

"I don't believe a word of it!" suddenly shrieked Miss Block from behind the door. "I expect you rushed in and knocked the poor old woman down like you did me! I shouldn't be a bit surprised to hear that she was lying unconscious behind the counter at this very moment!"

Madge was dreadfully disappointed by this fresh outbreak. She had hoped, judging by Miss Block's momentary calm, that she was becoming more reasonable, and that the door might soon be unlocked without there being any danger of a policeman being summoned. But this last absurd accusation of injuring Mrs. Winter was the worst of all. It would clearly be extreme folly to release Miss Block while she was capable of such malicious misrepresentations.

"I can't let you out unless you promise solemnly on your word and honour not to tell anybody silly stories about my stealing, or hurting Mrs. Winter. As if I would do such a thing!" shouted Madge through the key-hole.

"Help! Fire! Murder! Thieves!" shrieked Miss Block in reply.

"If you go on making that noise I won't unlock the door at all until Mrs. Winter comes back," threatened Madge, rendered desperate by terror.

"You won't let me out, won't you? Then I'll smash everything in this room with the poker!" screamed Miss Block in a voice choking with rage.

There was an ominous pause followed by a loud crash.

"Oh, please don't break Mrs. Winter's things! Please don't!" implored Madge. "It isn't her fault, you know, or mine either for the matter of that! The whole thing is a mistake, just because you won't listen to the true—"

"I am going to wait exactly one minute," interrupted Miss Block, "and at the end of that time if the door isn't opened I shall knock the clock off the chimney-piece, and the glass shade that is over it too!"

Poor Madge was almost wild with terror at this horrid threat. She broke out into incoherent cries and entreaties for mercy, to which there was no reply. Then she dashed to the street door in the hope of seeing Mrs. Winter, but only an unceasing flow of strangers passed along the pavement outside.

"The minute is over!" screamed Miss Block. "Let me out at once or—"

Madge was dreadfully afraid of a policeman, and felt that, very shortly, the worst terror of her life would come to pass and she would be dragged off to prison. Still, she could not let kind old Mrs. Winter's best clock be broken on her account. She unlocked the parlour door and flung it wide open.

Out bounded Miss Block, her face scarlet with rage, the pink hat cocked unbecomingly over one ear. "You miserable, impertinent, thieving little wretch!" she stammered, literally sobbing with fury. "I'll soon teach—"

"My dear child! What has happened, and what are you doing?" interrupted a calm voice.

Unnoticed by the two angry girls the street door had opened, and there stood Miss Thompson. When things came to be explained afterwards there was nothing very strange about her arriving at that moment, but to Madge her appearance seemed so opportune as to be little short of miraculous. In point of fact Miss Thompson had left the linen-draper's shortly before, and on looking up and down the street for her pupil had seen her face peeping out of Mrs. Winter's door. Madge at the time had been so occupied in watching for Mrs. Winter that she had no thoughts to spare for anyone else, and never noticed Miss Thompson until she heard her voice.

Miss Block was not at the best of times a well-bred girl, and now, her face distorted with passion she seemed ready, positively, to fly at Madge. Anything like opposition or argument would have produced a regular torrent of rude words and foolish accusations. But Miss Thompson did not give her any chance of being insulting; she was so calm herself, and so full of dignified apologies for Madge's behaviour, that before long the angry girl left off sobbing hysterically and began to listen to reason.

When Miss Block had heard the whole story she felt distinctly uncomfortable. Captain West was exceedingly well known in the neighbourhood, and the last thing Miss Block would have wished to do was to call his daughter a thief; but how could she guess that a plainly-dressed little girl in a small shop belonged to anyone of importance? Miss Block was sufficiently vulgar to have different manners for different classes of society. It confused her very much to find that she had treated Captain West's daughter as if she were Mrs. Winter's grandchild, or even someone poorer.

"Well, I'm very sorry for all that's happened," she said awkwardly. "It's been a mistake, and I hope Captain West won't think any more about it." Miss Thompson politely assured her that Captain West would attach no importance to the unpleasant interview that had taken place between his daughter and Miss Block, in fact that he would probably never hear of it.

"That's a good thing!" cried Miss Block, evidently much relieved by this assurance. "Then I think I'll be going. And," she added, pausing for a moment in the doorway, "there's not much fear of my coming here again! I might have guessed something would happen in a low little place like this! None of these vulgar poky shops for me in future!"

Miss Thompson was about to speak rather sharply in defence of Mrs. Winter, when Miss Block cut her short by flouncing noisily out of the shop.

There was a short silence, and then Miss Thompson said: "I need not point out to you, Madge, the extreme vulgarity of that last remark?"

"About the poky little shop, do you mean?" asked Madge shyly.

"Yes, indeed. I doubt whether anybody has ever before behaved half so rudely in this little house as the smartly-dressed girl who has just gone out of it. I am glad to see, however, that she has not really broken anything in the parlour, only knocked over a small table to try and frighten you with the noise. But we won't talk of her any more." And Miss Thompson shrugged her shoulders impatiently.

Fortunately, at this point Mrs. Winter returned, bringing with her the key of the empty house that she had actually persuaded the caretaker to lend her.

"I have promised faithfully to return it to him this evening, miss," said the kind old woman. "He made some little difficulties at first about letting it go out of his own hands, but being in the shoe-making business he couldn't come himself till after work hours, and I told him the young lady was in a sad way to be getting home again before tea-time—"

"I don't think the young lady is half as anxious to get home in good time as I am!" laughed Miss Thompson. Then she thanked Mrs. Winter heartily for the trouble she had taken to get back the children's money. "And now that we have the key," she concluded, "it will soon be recovered. I will stay in the shop, and if any customers come I will ask them to wait a few minutes until Mrs. Winter returns."

Madge was quite satisfied with this arrangement; she had had enough of keeping shop for one afternoon. Besides, she was very anxious to see the inside of the empty house.

CHAPTER XVII
IN AN EMPTY HOUSE

It was with a certain air of importance that Mrs. Winter walked along the pavement, closely followed by Madge. The friendly old woman always took a great interest in her neighbours' affairs, and she thoroughly enjoyed seeing the recovery of the lost money with her own eyes. When, after about a dozen steps, the front-door of the adjoining house was reached, Mrs. Winter smiled with conscious pride as she put the key into the key-hole. It was a critical moment. If the children ever recovered their lost money it would be entirely owing to her exertions. Not many elderly women in Churchbury that afternoon were playing such an exciting part.

The street in which Mrs. Winter lived was an old one, and consequently built without any regularity. It thus happened that next to Mrs. Winter's tiny shop stood a substantial family dwelling-house, whose cellars, as it has been said, took up rather more room on the pavement than seemed rightly to belong to them. Since the death of the last occupant some time before, the house had stood empty; only the caretaker visited it occasionally to air the rooms.

When Mrs. Winter pushed the heavy, creaking front-door open Madge followed her into a roomy hall, out of which a handsome staircase led to the upper part of the house. It was all very dignified and dreary. When the door was shut the noise echoed all over the house. It was not a very cheerful sound, especially heard in the sombre twilight caused by windows with the blinds all drawn down.

"We shall want a light for the cellar," observed Mrs. Winter. "The man said I should find all that was required on the window-sill in the hall—and here it is too!" she continued joyfully, holding up as she spoke a box of matches and a short candle stuck in a bottle.

Madge was exceedingly interested in this simple form of candlestick, and asked permission to carry it, in spite of the grease trickling down the bottle on to her fingers at every draught, as soon as the candle was lighted.

"It's a fine house. I've been over it many a time in old Doctor Freeman's day," said Mrs. Winter thoughtfully. "But it isn't much to see now since the sale, with all the furniture gone out of the rooms and the carpets up. Besides, we have not the time to lose going over it, or the lady will get tired of waiting for you."

Madge always liked investigating unknown places and things, but still she could not deny that Miss Thompson was awaiting her return rather anxiously. And when Mrs. Winter, taking another key fully as large as the first, proceeded to push open a heavy door and disclose a steep flight of slippery stone steps leading downwards into the cellars, Madge had the comfort of feeling that at all events she was seeing the most interesting part of the house. The bedrooms, or even attics, could not be as thrilling as that yawning chasm beneath her feet into which she was now about to plunge.

"Poor old Doctor Freeman set a great store on his collection of wine," observed Mrs. Winter as she slowly went down the cellar steps, feeling with her hands along the wall, for the bit of candle that Madge carried in front gave a very insufficient light, and she was terribly afraid of slipping. However, her nervousness did not prevent her from giving Madge a long account of the sale that had taken place after Dr. Freeman's death, and of the large sums of money that people gave for his treasured collections of wine.

"And to my thinking he would have been much wiser to drink it himself, poor gentleman!" she concluded. "But each one knows what he likes best, and if he preferred the look of the bottles to the taste of what was in them—well, 'twas his own to do what he liked with!"

Madge did not listen very attentively to Mrs. Winter's somewhat rambling discourse. By this time they had reached the bottom step, and another large key having been produced the last heavy door was opened with a loud creak. To any young lady who had read as many fairy-tales as Madge, the situation irresistibly suggested a subterranean cavern, in which unlimited gold was stored away by thrifty dwarfs.

"And there really is a lot of money there," thought Madge; "five shillings and sevenpence might easily be called a heap of treasure—with a little pretending. But I do wish Betty and John were here to help to discover it! We should have so much more fun."

Mrs. Winter was not a very satisfactory companion on an adventurous expedition. She was kindness itself—nobody could have been more good-natured,—but she did not seem quite to enter into the spirit of the thing. The dark mysterious cavern remained to her nothing but Dr. Freeman's empty wine-cellar; and it evidently never occurred to her for a moment that there was anything to be gained by calling the candle-end a torch! Life in the nursery and schoolroom at home had afforded Madge comparatively few opportunities for real adventure; and when one suddenly fell across her path it was tiresome to have an unappreciative companion who took everything as a matter of course.

Presently a trifling accident brought about a change in the situation. At the farther end of the long cellar there was a very faint glimmer of light coming through a grating overhead.

"That's where your money dropped down," observed Mrs. Winter. "You are sure to find it scattered on the ground under the grating."

At this suggestion Madge very naturally ran forward, and the violent draught coming from the opening above blew out the candle she carried in her hand.

Poor Mrs. Winter was greatly disturbed by suddenly finding herself in the dark. Even by the light of the candle it had seemed hard work to her coming down the steep steps, and how she was ever to get up them again in total darkness she really did not know. Yet she would not consent to let Madge go back to the hall where the matches had had been left and light the candle, fearing that the little girl might set fire to the house.

"Then I may stay here in the dark by myself while you go, may I?" pleaded Madge, who did not wish to waste a minute of her time in this exciting place.

"Yes, I suppose so," replied Mrs. Winter, rather wondering at the little girl's taste, but too much occupied in the effort of feeling her way to the stairs to pay much attention to anything else. Presently she could be heard slowly mounting step by step, then the door at the top of the stairs shut with a noisy clang behind her, and there was silence.

Madge was all alone in the dark. It was certainly delightfully exciting, but not, strictly speaking, quite so enjoyable as she had anticipated. The chief pleasure would be in afterwards describing to Betty and John what had happened. In the meantime she would be very brave, and Mrs. Winter might return at any moment with the candle.

The worst of darkness and silence is, that they seem to increase every moment. What is merely gloomy at first becomes almost intolerable as time goes on. All sorts of horrid ideas came into Madge's head. Could it be that Mrs. Winter had shut her in and gone home? Or fallen down in a fit in the hall? Or that the cellar door had slammed with a spring-lock and could not be got open again? None of these suppositions would have seemed very probable in the light; but Madge was becoming too frightened to form a clear judgment on the subject. She longed to call out in the hopes of getting an answer from Mrs. Winter, but dread of hearing her own voice echoing through the empty house kept her silent. And from the same cause she remained standing motionless on the spot where she had been left. The terror of stepping on some strange soft object that would squeak or squash under her feet was enough to keep her still. She thought of Lewis Brand's tales about rats and toads in Mrs. Howard's cellar, and she wondered that he did not go mad when shut up among them.

As Madge was standing stiff with fright, and straining her ears to catch a distant sound of footsteps that never seemed to come, she suddenly remembered the grating at the farther end of the cellar. "What a stupid creature I am!" she exclaimed joyfully, as, turning her head, she again caught sight of the reassuring glimmer of light behind her. It had been there all the time, while she was staring into the darkness in the opposite direction.

In another moment Madge was cautiously creeping towards the grating. She could only go slowly pushing one foot before her in order to avoid stepping heavily on some hidden horror; for the daylight struggling through the tiny opening overhead only faintly lighted the ground immediately below, leaving the rest of the cellar in total darkness.

Even this feeble patch of twilight quite restored Madge's confidence. She would reach it and feel about for the lost money, then if Mrs. Winter did not speedily return she could no doubt find her way back up the cellar steps without any help. When Madge was not frightened she was just as sensible and energetic as a grown-up person.

Hardly had she resolved on this most practical course, however, when there was a wild scuffle round her legs, and something brushed past her with glaring eyes—something that uttered confused sounds of rage as it lurked in the darkness to spring out upon her.

Poor Madge! She forgot her age, her dignity, and her character for good common sense. She only remembered alarming stories about hobgoblins and witches, and she began to scream. Luckily Mrs. Winter had by this time found the box of matches, and very soon returned with the candle. Then all at once the scene changed. The mysterious haunted cavern again became nothing but a large cellar full of empty shelves, hung with festoons of cobwebs. And the lurking monster turned out to be a half-starved kitten, that must at some time have followed the caretaker down the steps and got locked in.

With trembling hands and a rather shamefaced expression Madge collected the fallen coins, many of which had rolled out of the bag to some distance. She could not bear to think that Mrs. Winter had heard her screaming like a frightened baby. The annoyance of this recollection prevented her from taking any interest in the poor kitten that Mrs. Winter was gently coaxing towards her; and it was not until they were again back in the little shop that Madge regained her customary good spirits.

CHAPTER XVIII
THE RETURN AFTER SHOPPING

After all, there was very little time left for the important work of choosing toys. Madge did her best to make up her mind in a hurry, assisted by a good deal of judicious advice from Miss Thompson. But that was not the way in which she enjoyed shopping. She liked to dwell on every purchase, carefully calculating whether its merits justified its price, and trying to imagine how it would look when the stuffing came out of it, or the paint was rubbed off. When the money was not all her own, and the toys not all for herself, as in the present instance, it naturally much increased the difficulty of selection. There were the tastes and needs of different people to be considered, their various wants and wishes to be recalled. Madge was a most conscientious shopper, and in the main a thoughtful elder sister. She would have scorned to spend Betty's and John's money and not give them full satisfaction.

"My dear child," said Miss Thompson at last, "I have really waited as long as I dare. We must go to the place where we left the carriage, and start home. Your parents will think we have met with an accident."

"Oh, please wait a minute! Just one minute!" begged Madge. "I haven't half chosen yet. That's to say, I have put together a lot of things that might do, but I want to look through them before I quite settle."

"Perhaps I can help you to decide?" said Miss Thompson briskly. "What's this? A whip and a boat for John? Surely that is exactly what he had last time we went shopping?"

"Yes; but he has broken the old whip, and he wants another boat," explained Madge. "They have just put such a nice great tub of water in the garden, because the pump has gone dry with the hot weather, and we sail—"

"Oh, that's all right!" interrupted Miss Thompson. "So long as you know what you like and are satisfied. And Betty is to have this doll, I suppose, and that trumpet? Isn't she getting rather old for a trumpet?"

"But she likes a trumpet better than anything, except a whistle," explained Madge hurriedly. "We all like trumpets or anything that makes a noise."

"You are welcome to your noises so long as I hear nothing of them in the schoolroom!" laughed Miss Thompson. "And you have chosen a knife and a china tea-pot for yourself, I see. Well, now be quick and let Mrs. Winter make up the bill."

"But there was a lot of other little things I want to get!" cried Madge. "I have not had time to think properly yet."

Miss Thompson looked at her watch, and said that she would wait exactly five minutes and no more. At the end of that period Madge with many groans of regret was obliged to turn away from the counter, feeling that if she only had all the time she wanted she would immediately put back most of the things she had chosen and select fresh ones. Perhaps it was just as well that she was rather hurried, for at this rate there would have been no end to the shopping.

Mrs. Winter parted from her customers with many invitations to them to return and see how the poor half-starved kitten prospered under her care. She had already put him to bed in a basket in the back-kitchen, after giving him two whole saucers of milk, that he drank without stopping. Altogether it seemed probable that he would find the shop a much more agreeable residence than the cellar, where, judging by the prominence of his ribs, he must have kept himself alive on a very limited supply of mice and black-beetles.

It was long past the usual time for schoolroom tea when Miss Thompson and Madge returned home. The twins, it may be remembered, had been climbing in the Eagle's Nest a good part of the afternoon, and were consequently as hungry as people who have been playing for hours in the open air have a right to be. They were waiting on the door-step when the carriage drove up, and began at once to reproach Madge for being so late, and to inquire what she had brought.

"Come along," said Miss Thompson briskly. "Not a word is to be spoken until Madge has taken off her hat and we are seated at the tea-table. If we begin to embark on our adventures now, we shall never get any tea to-night."

The children grumbled, but they were forced to obey, as Miss Thompson waited to see Madge walk upstairs before she took off her own jacket. Long experience had taught her that if an exciting story was once begun, even tea would be forgotten.

At last, however, the delightful moment had arrived, when the children were all seated round the table and at liberty to recount their afternoon's occupations. Of course, Madge's adventures were altogether so out of the common as to throw everything else into the shade. The twins said nothing about their meeting with Lewis, and Madge never thought of inquiring what they had been doing. They did not intentionally conceal anything, but in the excitement of hearing about the loss and recovery of the brown bag they completely forgot what, up to that time, had been a great source of pride—namely, that they had been associating on equal terms of friendship with a big school-boy. Even when tea was over and Miss Thompson left them alone, they forgot to tell Madge how they had spent the afternoon, in the interest of looking at the new purchases.

"Well, I suppose all's well that ends well," remarked Betty solemnly, as she helped to unpack the brown paper parcels on the schoolroom table. "Only it must have been very terrible in that cellar, especially when you saw those flaming eyes in the dark! What colour were they, green or yellow?"

"Oh, I hardly remember! The colour of cats' eyes, I suppose!" replied Madge rather impatiently.

She did not much care to dwell upon that time in the cellar, when she had mistaken the poor starved kitten for some sort of hobgoblin, and screamed at it in a way that was most unworthy of her age and good sense. To change the subject, she asked John how he liked the things she had chosen for him.

"The ship is all right," he said slowly, "and so is the whip. At least it's not quite so big as the one I got last time, and it cost a penny more, but still it will do. Only—"

"Well, what's the matter?" interrupted Madge. "What have you got to grumble at now, I should like to know?"

She spoke sharply, for, with all her kindness, she could not bear to have the younger ones finding fault with anything she did. So long as they were duly grateful she would work hard to amuse them; but the moment they began to criticise her conduct in any way there was trouble.

"Do you think you could have chosen anything better yourself?" she said scornfully. "You had better try next time if you think it's so easy!"

"I didn't say the things were not nice things," observed John in his quiet obstinate way. "I never meant that. Only I can't understand how you spent our money. That's all."

"Why it's as simple as A B C!" broke out Madge. "Just listen, you little silly, and I'll tell you. I took five shillings and sevenpence, didn't I?"

"Of course you did! In the brown bag," answered Betty, although nobody had spoken to her.

John merely nodded his head to show that he was following the argument up to this point.

"And as the money belonged to us all we were all to share alike," proceeded Madge rapidly. "So I got a ship and a doll and a knife, each costing a shilling. And we had one apiece. That's three shillings. Then the whip and the trumpet and the tea-pot cost sixpence each. That comes to four shillings and sixpence. And the packets of sugar-plums, and pipes for blowing soap-bubbles, come to tenpence. That makes five shillings and four-pence. And—and—"

"And that's all!" interrupted John. "But you took five shillings and sevenpence in the brown bag, you know. I remember counting it; didn't we, Betty?"

"Oh, I'm well aware of that!" cried Madge impatiently. "If you will only just keep quiet I can make it right in a moment. I must have added up wrongly while you were chattering." And spreading all the purchases out on the table she tried to count them more carefully over again, repeating their prices as she did so. But it was no use. Try as she might her accounts would not come perfectly right. There was threepence missing, and Madge could not account for it at all.

"It must have slipped out of the bag and be lying in a corner of that cellar," said Betty with considerable reason. "Threepence is such a very tiny bit of money you would never see it in the dark, or even by the light of one candle."

"Perhaps not. I suppose that is what has happened," admitted poor Madge. She was ready to cry with mortification at having had the worst of the argument with John, in spite of his being two years younger than herself and very much her inferior in arithmetic. Besides, she knew that if she had, as seemed most probable, left a threepenny piece on the cellar floor, it was all owing to that annoying fit of nervousness that had suddenly come over her in the dark. At the time that she picked up the money she was still suffering from the fright caused by the sudden appearance of the kitten, and no doubt had been too much upset to notice very carefully what she was doing. But she did not like to explain all this to the twins, who were in the habit of looking upon her as the living embodiment of courage. So she merely laid the blame on the dim light of the cellar.

The consequence of this was, that when John next found himself alone with Betty he began to grumble.

"It's all very well for Madge to say she didn't see the threepenny bit," he said, "but I think she ought to have stayed there looking until she did see it. She can see things very well when she tries. I don't believe she took any trouble about it, because it belonged to us."

"But part of it belonged to her," objected Betty.

"Only one part," said John persistently, "and two parts belonged to us. So of course it was more ours than hers, and that's why she didn't trouble to look for it."

"Do you think so really?" said Betty in an irresolute tone. She had great faith in Madge always acting for the best, but these new arguments were rather disturbing.

"I'll tell you what it is," continued John. "Madge thinks herself a much grander person than we are, because she is a little older. And it isn't fair. Lewis said he wouldn't be ordered about by her if he were in my place, and I won't either. After all, she is only a girl!"

After this remark the conversation became rather quarrelsome. Betty objected to the expression, "only a girl", and retorted by some very rude remarks about boys in general and her brother in particular. She reminded him with unpleasant emphasis of how slow he was at climbing trees compared with Madge, and she dwelt with more truth than politeness on the fact that he had once grown giddy on the roof of the cow-house, and had to be ignominiously helped down by his sisters. But in the long run John's solid persistency got the best of it, and in spite of Betty's wish to believe that Madge always acted for the best, she was gradually talked over into thinking that there was some real grievance in her elder sister always taking the lead.

Whenever Lewis Brand had an opportunity of talking to the twins by themselves he mischievously encouraged this idea, so that disagreements among the children became a matter of everyday occurrence.

CHAPTER XIX
AN INTERESTING DITCH

If a stranger had happened to meet Madge, Betty, and John one fine Saturday afternoon a few weeks later in the summer, he would probably have imagined that they were hurrying to the sea-side. It was certainly an odd way to get there, across the fields and through a grove of beech-trees; but where else could they be going, each carrying a boat?

They passed by the Eagle's Nest for once without even glancing up at it, and walking a little farther along the field stopped by a deep ditch. Now, even during the hottest summer weather this delightful ditch seldom became completely dry. A tiny stream generally contrived to trickle along the bottom, pushing its way in and out among the dead leaves and sticks that the wind blew into its course. During the winter months the ditch sometimes got blocked with this sort of rubbish, and then the water being kept back very rapidly rose and flooded over the field. However, old Barton was always on the look-out for accidents, and on extra wet days generally marched out with a sack over his shoulders to keep them comparatively dry, and cleared away the drifts of dead leaves with his spade so that the stream should flow freely. Of course, the children would have loved to accompany him on these expeditions, but they always took place on such wet days that the thing was not to be thought of seriously.

But though the children were never allowed to help in moderating a regular winter flood, they valued the ditch highly as a place where they could always collect enough water to sail their boats in a thoroughly satisfactory manner. They had done it so often that they did not take very long time in setting to work. Betty and John going down on their knees began to build the mud and dead leaves at the bottom of the ditch into a great barrier across the narrowest part, while Madge with a stick cleared the course of the stream from all obstructions above. It was the way in which they made tiny ponds in the cracks of the big stones under the laburnum-tree, only of course this was hundreds of times larger.

The water soon began to rise. It is most surprising what a lot of water even a tiny stream contains if one can once prevent it from all running away!

When the ditch was about half-full, the children launched their boats and made them go imaginary voyages from port to port, carrying merchandise.

"I will be London," said Madge, "and Betty can be Cardiff, and—"

"I can choose for myself without your help!" interrupted John peevishly. "I'll be Birmingham."

"Oh, you choose very cleverly for yourself!" jeered Madge. "I wonder how you can think of such difficult places!"

"You think nobody can be clever except yourself, but you are finely mistaken," rejoined John seriously; and he could not imagine why both his sisters burst out laughing. "There isn't much joke that I can see in that," he said.

"The joke is about Birmingham, you know," explained Betty. "It isn't a port."

"Then it ought to be," said John decidedly.

"Perhaps you had better write to the Queen and suggest that it should be made into one," remarked Madge. But then, seeing that her brother looked vexed at his mistake, she continued cheerfully: "I have thought of a new and much better plan. We will not have real towns, but we will call them after our own names—Madgebury, Bettybury, and Johnbury!"

This idea gave very general satisfaction, and the game proceeded most peacefully for some time. A vessel laden with acorns started from Madgebury and went to Johnbury, crossing on the way another ship full of horse-chestnuts. From Bettybury a small wooden doll set out on a voyage of discovery into unknown regions, the owners carefully superintending the course of their vessels and guiding them by long strings. Once the strings got entangled and there was a terrific shipwreck in Johnbury harbour, most of the cargo, consisting of marbles, being lost in the mud at the bottom. After this collision it was discovered that the sails of two of the vessels were injured, so the ship-owners decided to retire for a short time to Eagle's Nest and work at some necessary repairs.

It was a warm afternoon, and the shade of the great spreading beech-tree was particularly pleasant after an hour spent in the glaring sun by the ditch. The children sat about in idle lounging attitudes, mending their boats and talking in a leisurely fashion.

"I wish I hadn't lost all those marbles," remarked John mournfully. "I only found four, and I believe there were quite eight in the ship, only the mud was so soft they sank out of sight at once. I squeezed it all over with my hands to try and find them, but I couldn't."

"I should think you will lose those four as well, if you try and carry them in your pocket," said Madge. "Don't you remember what a big hole you have in it, and how your knife dropped on the schoolroom floor this morning when you were saying your lessons?"

"But I must put them somewhere," answered John peevishly. "I can't leave them behind, and I can't carry them in my hand when I am mending my ship."

"I've got a capital idea!" broke in Betty. "We will have a treasure-house in the Eagle's Nest, and we can safely hide away the things we don't want there. And I see just the place that will do!" With an excited cry she scrambled up to a hole in the tree a few feet above the platform of sticks on which they sat. "Isn't this the very place?" she shouted.

"The very place! The very place!" echoed John; and immediately the three children began to empty out their pockets and decide what they would leave in the Eagle's Nest storehouse. John's marbles and various small articles belonging to the girls, such as pencils, both slate and lead, a broken knife, and a doll's boot, were carefully stored away packed in dock leaves.

"We can leave them there all right," said Madge. "Even if it rains they can't get wet in this beautiful hole. It's a regular out-of-door cupboard, and I shall keep lots of my things here now that we have found it."

This plan was so incomparably more interesting than putting one's possessions back tamely in the schoolroom or nursery, that the hole was soon filled with oddly-shaped parcels tied up in leaves and twists of grass.

"That's done!" exclaimed Madge at last with a sigh of satisfaction, as she covered the opening to the hole with an enormous bunch of elder flowers, which she fondly hoped looked so natural that no passing enemy would suspect they concealed a treasure-house. "Now shall we go back and sail our boats or—Oh, look!" her voice rose to a shriek. And well it might.

Quite taken up with their present occupation, the children had entirely forgotten the fact that they had left the ditch blocked, so that the stream could not flow away as usual. The water had been rising for the last hour or more, and all one end of the field was rapidly turning into a swamp. Rivulets of water were finding their way in and out among the rank tufts of long grass, and at this rate Eagle's Nest itself would be surrounded by the evening.

It was a moment of most intense excitement. There were hurried consultations among the children, and even a daring suggestion that the flood should be allowed to rise until they were left upon an impregnable island. But a certain longing for tea, combined with a wholesome dread of Barton, prevented this alarmingly bold scheme from being carried out.

"If we had only known what was going to happen and brought provisions with us, what fun it would have been to stay here all night!" cried Madge, who dearly loved an adventure. "I think if I had brought the piece of bread that they put by the side of my plate at dinner, and that I never eat, it would have been enough to keep me alive all night."

"I should like sandwiches better," observed John.

"Very likely!" rejoined Madge impatiently. "Honey and cream are very nice too, and just what people always carry with them when they are out all night in a forest!"

"They would be very good, but much stickier than sandwiches," began John, then stopped as both his sisters burst out laughing. "I don't see anything funny," he said sulkily. "They are very sticky, you know they are!"

"We were laughing at your idea of having all sorts of nice things to eat when you were escaping from the enemy," explained Betty. "It's a time for hardships—"

"I don't care to live on hardships," interrupted John.

"Well, it doesn't matter, because I think we had better go home to tea after all," observed Madge. "I don't really mind Barton complaining about us much; and it would have been frightful fun to sit in the Eagle's Nest and see everybody on the other side of the water scolding and threatening us without being able to get at us. But I dare say Mama would have been rather anxious about our staying out all night in the damp."

Though troublesome and thoughtless the children were really affectionate, and this consideration weighed with them. They gave up all idea of allowing the advancing torrent to cut them off from any communication with the world. (When we talk of the torrent, it must be understood that it might not have appeared quite worthy of the name to grown-up people; but that is how the children managed to see it.)

Having decided to resist the temptation of camping-out for a night, the next question was how to avoid getting into serious trouble with Barton, who would be dreadfully cross if he came in the morning and found the field turned into a swamp. It was all very well for Madge to talk defiantly about not minding if Barton scolded or not; but the fact was that everybody, even Captain West, stood in respectful awe of the old man's stern disapproval.

"I do wish you children would not be so disobedient to me before Barton. I can see he thinks you are spoilt, and it makes me feel so dreadfully ashamed of myself!" Captain West would laughingly say; and though, of course, this was only a joke, there can be little doubt that Barton would have brought up a family very strictly if it had been left to him.

"We can't go home and leave it like this," said Madge, looking round despairingly on the ever-widening circle of glistening wet that was spreading through the grass.

"If we took away the mud that we put across the ditch, would not the stream run down the ditch again as usual?" suggested John.

"Of course, we all know that! But who can get through the water to clear it out?" cried Betty.

There was an anxious pause. Then suddenly in a tone of solemn resolution Madge announced that she was once more ready to take the post of danger.

"You will get your boots wet through, and catch cold," said Betty nervously.

Without replying to this remonstrance Madge climbed down from the Eagle's Nest. It was the work of a moment to remove not only her boots but also her stockings. Then she plunged into the soaking grass, the water splashing up round her bare feet at every step. It was a wet job, and a dirty one, but Madge accomplished it safely, and Barton never guessed next day how near he had been to finding the meadow flooded.

CHAPTER XX
DISPUTES

The treasure-house in Eagle's Nest did not turn out quite such a happy idea as was anticipated. For a few days after causing the ditch to overflow the children rather avoided that part of the fields. It seemed prudent not to give Barton any occasion to connect them in his mind with the extra muddiness of the corner between Eagle's Nest and the ditch. But when nearly a week had passed by without any awkward inquiries being made, and it was considered safe to return to their old haunts, an unpleasant surprise awaited them. Some of their carefully-stored-away possessions were missing!

John's marbles could nowhere be found. This was a most unfortunate fact; but when, after a hurried turning out of the contents of the treasure-house, it became apparent that a pencil also belonging to John was missing, there was a positive uproar. Betty had only lost an old pocket-book with all the leaves torn out, and she was not even quite sure that she had ever put it into the hole. Madge had lost nothing.

"I do say it's a shame!" shouted John positively, dancing about on the platform of the Eagle's Nest with rage. "It's a horrid shame! All my things are lost, and—"

"If you stamp so hard your foot will stick in the cracks of the floor, like the dwarf in the fairy-story," interrupted Madge.

"Oh, it's all very well to laugh! Laugh away!" shouted John. "That's just like you! Put in all your own things safely enough, and left mine out! And then you laugh. But I won't stand being bullied by a great ugly thing—" Here his voice fortunately became choked with angry sobs.

"What is the matter? What nonsense you are talking!" exclaimed Madge impatiently. "All the things were put into the hole at the same time. You saw me do it yourself, because I happened to be nearest to the treasure-house."

"And I believe I saw you pushing my things on one side to make room for your own!" rejoined John. "And very likely you slily took some of mine out and threw them away, so that the hole should not be too full."

"Well, if you believe all that you must be a little idiot!" said Madge scornfully; and Betty cried: "How can you say such things? Of course she wouldn't!"

"I think she would," asserted John, with irritating obstinacy. "She thinks she can do as she likes with us and our things. Lewis often says—"

"So it is Lewis who has been putting all these stupid ideas into your head?" interrupted Madge. "I could not think why you had become so discontented and grumbling all of a sudden! Now I see what it is, and I'll never speak to that sneak again!"

"He is a very nice boy, very nice indeed," repeated John. "And I like talking to him much better than playing with girls."

"You are welcome to him, I'm sure!" exclaimed Madge tempestuously. "A horrid sneak who used to be always laughing at you little ones to me, and calling you silly babies! And then directly my back is turned for an afternoon, he goes trying to set you against me. No, I don't want him coming sucking up to me any more, that's certain!" And a good deal more of the same sort; for when Madge was indignant, she had an extraordinary flow of very forcible but inelegant language. "Now for my part I'm going away from here directly," she concluded. "John will stop and tell tales to his friend, I suppose. Betty can do as she likes."

Betty did not look as grateful as she might for this kind permission. She was a peace-loving little person, and always particularly disliked being called upon to take sides in family disputes.

"Can't we all go away and play together just as we used to, before we knew Lewis?" she said at last. "We really had more fun then than we have now, because we were not always afraid that something would be found out."

"You are quite right!" answered Madge heartily. "We built this Eagle's Nest to play in, didn't we? But now, instead of playing we are always watching and waiting for Lewis, and when he comes we can't have any fun, because if we make a noise somebody may catch us. It seems rather a sneaking business altogether."

Betty was quite of this opinion. If she had not been drawn on by her elder sister's enthusiasm in the first instance, she would never have done anything so boldly naughty as to make friends with a strange boy. The constant fear of discovery had weighed heavily upon her, and on more than one occasion lately she had trembled all over if anyone had called her suddenly, thinking that the whole affair was discovered and she was about to be blamed. "Yes, do let us play somewhere else. And then perhaps Lewis will get tired of coming to look for us," she said fervently.

"At first I was sorry for him," continued Madge, "and I should be now, only he is so mean. Of course I shall never betray him to anybody, and get him punished for climbing over the wall. But I won't speak to him after he has proved a sneak!"

In the end Madge and Betty went off together to play elsewhere, while John remained behind in the Eagle's Nest, saying that he should wait there for his friend. But it was not very cheerful work sitting alone on a bough in sight of that terrible red brick house, after the girls had disappeared. He would gladly have climbed down and ran after them, if he had not boasted so loudly of his preference for Lewis's society. And when Lewis at last came he was not a very cheery companion. John tried to feel flattered at being left alone with such a big boy, and to get all the comfort he could out of his companion's abuse of girls in general, and Madge in particular. But when Lewis began to tell long dreary stories about the cruel doings that went on under Mrs. Howard's roof, the small listener soon realized that the presence of a strong and courageous elder sister would be very comforting indeed. He tried to keep up his spirits by reflecting that there was no fear of his being entrapped from the Beechgrove side of the wall.

"Ah! Don't you make too sure of that," said Lewis. "The last boy Mrs. Howard stole was bigger than you, I think."

"Does she steal children, then?" cried John in terrified accents. "I didn't know anybody could do that nowadays! Why don't the police stop her?"

"That's just the question! My belief is that she's more artful than a whole army of police," answered Lewis. "I don't know how it's done of course, but I expect that man with a gray beard wanders about the road after dark and catches them as they are going home from school, perhaps in the evening—"

"Catches them? What does he catch?" interrupted John.

"Why, catches boys about your size, of course! I've just said so, haven't I? How stupid you are!" answered Lewis, speaking quite as contemptuously as Madge in her most overbearing moods. "And then they are locked into the cellars under the house.—Chained? Oh yes! hand and foot. Gags in their mouths too, if they groan loudly enough to be heard. I know the sound when I am awake at night. Mrs. Howard calls it the wind in the chimneys, but I know better than that."

"But what does she want boys for?" asked John in a trembling voice.

"Nobody knows. Perhaps she sells them as slaves to the black people, just as black people used to be sold to white. Perhaps she keeps them prisoners for life in her cellars. Nobody knows." Lewis began to whistle, and positively declined to give any further information.

"I think I'll go home, it's getting rather late," said John presently. "And very likely I sha'n't be able to come here to-morrow to meet you. It doesn't seem quite safe to come every day if that dreadful man is always on the look-out. Besides, I don't think I shall have much time after lessons, some days we dig in our gardens."

"You aren't afraid to come without your sisters, I suppose? It looks remarkably like it," said Lewis disagreeably.

"No! of course not!" cried John, as he hurriedly scrambled out of the tree.

In another moment he was in full flight home. It did not require much persuasion on Betty's part that evening to convince him that, after all, one's own brothers and sisters are much safer and pleasanter companions than any chance strangers.

"But," concluded Betty, "though Lewis talks so much about the dangers he goes through I don't believe he is half as brave as Madge. See how she plunged into that water the other day without hesitating an instant, though it was very cold, for my hands were quite blue after sailing my boat. It's so odd how water keeps cold even in the summer! But I don't think Lewis could have done it. He made such a fuss when he scratched his hand with a sharp stone in the wall one day. Of course he is very brave about being shut up in those dreadful cellars; only I don't think they can be quite so dreadful as he pretends, or nobody could bear them."

"Don't you think it is quite true about the cellars, then?" asked John, eagerly grasping at a ray of hope. If the cellars were not dungeons swarming with toads, then there might also be some mistake about little boys being stolen and sold as slaves to black people. So he waited anxiously for Betty's opinion on the subject.

"Well, I suppose it is true that he is shut up in those dark places," she replied thoughtfully; "because, you see, he can tell us all about them; the slimy walls I mean, and the black pools of dirty water. Only I don't believe he is quite as brave as he makes out. I dare say he cries and screams when he is locked in."

This answer did not do much to calm John's fears. After some natural hesitation at owning himself in the wrong, he said shyly:

"I don't think I care so very much about Lewis after all. He bullies just as much as Madge, and doesn't play such amusing games either."

"No, indeed he doesn't!" chimed in Betty eagerly. "It was much more amusing before we knew him, and there was no hiding things and being afraid of being found out. It doesn't seem right when we are trusted to go out by ourselves—"

"Oh, I don't know about that!" interrupted John. "I can't see any harm in it, not for me at least, because I am a boy, and boys don't stop to ask whether they may speak to people. I dare say you and Madge ought not to have done it, as you are girls. But," he added, rather less grandly, "I think I will play with you to-morrow instead of going to talk to Lewis. That's to say, I will come if Madge won't be nasty and disagreeable."

"Of course she won't! I'll talk to her about it, and she will be right enough when she hears you are not going to follow Lewis any more!" cried Betty, rejoicing in the prospect of the good time coming when they would once more all three play harmoniously together, without the interference of any mischief-making stranger.

CHAPTER XXI
OLD GAMES

It was many weeks since the children had started out in such high spirits as they did on the following afternoon. As long as they were secretly meeting Lewis, there was always a certain mystery about their doings which, though at first very exciting, soon became oppressive. They were in the main truthful, straightforward children, and when they were tempted first to talk to Lewis, and then to promise secrecy about having done so, they had not foreseen what an amount of concealment this conduct would give rise to in the future. Often when chattering about their doings before Miss Thompson or their parents, references to Lewis and his wonderful tales nearly slipped out, and the subject had to be awkwardly changed. Once or twice questions were asked to which the children, though they avoided telling downright falsehoods in reply, yet gave wilfully misleading answers. And they had been sufficiently well brought-up for this course of little deceptions to make them feel thoroughly uncomfortable.

It was a real relief to have done with Lewis and all concealment, and to be starting off boldly to play their old games, which, though a little noisy and rough, were admittedly innocent. Sometimes they were explorers discovering the source of the Nile; another day they would be an eager party of adventurers hunting for gold in Australia. In either case they carried long sticks and shouted the whole time. To-day, as it happened, they were big-game hunters, looking out for giraffes, elephants, and an occasional lion. They expected to find them behind the hay-ricks or in the poultry-yard; failing those likely spots, they would try the cow-house.

"I hope my new rifle will act to-day," observed Madge, shouldering a pea-stick with great dignity. "Last time I was out it missed fire, and I lost a fine buck in the forest."

This piece of information was received with perfect gravity by the other children. The only way to enjoy games properly is to be quite serious about them.

"I have slain twenty wolves with this spear!" cried John suddenly.

"But that's no reason why you should poke my eye out with it!" exclaimed Betty, seizing the rough end of a long stick that was being brandished close to her head.

"Oh, I'm so sorry! Your cheek is bleeding. Let's look!" and John proceeded to examine his handiwork with more apparent interest than regret.

"It's nothing! A miss is as good as a mile!" answered Betty impatiently, as she scrubbed her cheek with a dirty handkerchief. It was considered a great breach of etiquette to acknowledge that one was hurt when playing a game. At lessons, on the contrary, a little fuss about a scratch or bruise was allowable, because it took up time which otherwise would have been devoted to study.

"Hist! Go gently! We are tracking the wild boar to his lair!" muttered Madge. "Conceal yourselves from view behind the brushwood and creep after me."

Now, a mere ordinary grown-up person would have been puzzled how to carry out this order in a field where the grass was only about an inch long. He would have looked in vain for any shelter behind which even to hide his boots; he would in fact have been deplorably dense and literal. The three children did not hesitate for a minute. They slouched their hats forward over their faces, that being a concealment behind which it was recognized that no wild boar would be likely to penetrate; and they bent their knees into a fancied imitation of the attitude of an Indian on the war-path. This was the established mode of attacking a herd of wild animals.

"Halt! They have caught sight of us! Make ready your weapons!" cried Madge in a sort of suppressed shout. "They are preparing to charge! Look out!"

If the six black Berkshire pigs lying asleep in the sun under the wall were really preparing to charge they dissembled their purpose remarkably well. Half opening their tiny eyes they blinked lazily at their assailants, and it was not until they had received several sharp pokes from the long sticks that they would move from the spot where they were lying. Even then they only tottered a few steps farther off, and sank down again in a great heaving sleepy mass.

"If we threw a few stones at them perhaps they would run?" suggested John.

"Better not," said Madge; "supposing Barton saw us he would be sure to say we were hurting them."

"I only meant small ones, of course," answered John; "but I dare say he would make a fuss and tell Papa some long story, just as he did about our hunting the cows when we were only trying to catch the calf. He always thinks things are so much worse than they are really. But how shall we move the pigs without stones?"

Even Madge could not suggest a remedy for the pigs' excessive drowsiness. Words, or rather shouts, seemed thrown away upon their dull ears, and more active interference was impossible with Barton hovering in the neighbourhood. The chase threatened to come to a stand-still, when Betty burst into an agitated war-cry.

"The enemy are upon us! No, I forgot! The elephants, I mean! They are galloping towards us! We shall be overwhelmed!"

She waved her stick defiantly as she screamed, in the spirit of one prepared to perish sooner than surrender.

This time the alarm had sufficient foundation in fact to be very exciting. A young heifer, attracted by the noise, and probably thinking that it had some connection with Barton and hay, set off trotting across the field, followed at a discreet pace by all the milking-cows. In the distance, with the help of a little imagination, they made quite a formidable array.

"We are outnumbered! There is no dishonour in flight!" shouted Madge in the grand phrases gained from books, that were always employed on these occasions. "Rush for the fort!" she continued. "The fort under the oak-tree!"

The children needed no further instructions. They had well-established settlements under several of the trees, consisting of fallen branches that had been chopped into logs and piled in a heap to remain there until wanted. In a few minutes more they were defying elephants and everything else from the summit of a log-pile fully five feet high, their backs planted firmly against the solid trunk of the oak-tree. So safe did they feel that it was annoying of the cows not to come on faster, and they took it as nothing short of a direct insult when the leading heifer, to whom they had all along alluded as a mad bull, gave up the pursuit and began quietly to eat.

"There's no spirit in anything, elephants or bulls! I never saw anything like it!" said Madge in a tone of utter disgust. "If they won't run away how can one hunt them?"

"But what is that coming in and out of the farmyard doorway? It isn't there always," said John, screwing up his eyes and trying to see across the field in the blinding sunshine.

"I think it's a dog! I am almost sure it is," observed Betty nervously. "I do hope it is not a mad dog that has strayed in off the road."

"That's not very likely," laughed Madge. "There aren't many mad dogs on the road, in fact I know people are obliged to keep them shut up at home, or muzzled, or—"

"Yes, I dare say that is the rule. But suppose this one had escaped without anybody noticing him?" said Betty, who was very much afraid of dogs; "and suppose he smelt us out, and followed us down here?"

"Well, I should just pat him on the head," said Madge loftily. "You can make friends with any dog if you aren't afraid of him."

"I say!" exclaimed John suddenly. "It's that brute belonging to the butcher, that bit the postman. He is wandering about the field, I can see him quite plainly. The butcher must be in the yard talking to Barton about buying the calf. I think we had better run back to the house." Even the courageous Madge prepared to act on this suggestion. They had been warned never to go near the butcher's dog, and it really seemed almost beyond the bounds of sport to wait patiently until he chose to bite them.

"We will run for the house!" cried Madge, rather enjoying the excitement. "Now, off!"

As is often the case, Betty, being the most nervous and anxious to get away, made a false start, her foot slipped between two logs of wood and remained firmly jammed. "Oh stop! stop!" she cried, as the others, not noticing her misfortune, were hurrying away across the field in the direction of home. "I can't get out! Don't run away!" she wailed frantically, twisting and tugging at her foot, but only succeeding in hurting her ankle rather severely.

The large dog, who had up to this time contented himself with sniffing about at the top of the field near the yard where his master was standing, being attracted by the noise now began prowling like a wolf nearer and nearer to the oak-tree. Betty, looking up from an ineffectual struggle to roll the logs farther apart, saw him half-way across the field towards her, and gave a terrific scream.

"What's that?" cried Madge, checking herself and looking back. "Why, Betty has never come! What's the matter?" While speaking she had turned and was rushing back towards her younger sister.

"The dog is coming! Look! He is coming!" shrieked Betty, almost frantic with fright.

"I'll keep him off! Trust me!" gasped Madge, breathless with running, as she posted herself in front of the logs, waving her stick like a battle-axe. Her courage was undeniable, and fortunately her strength was not put to any proof, as the butcher, hearing terrified cries, stepped outside the yard and whistled to his dog.

"There! it has turned round! It is running back to its master! Barton is there, so he will take care that it doesn't follow us again. I dare say it would not have bitten, though," said Madge soothingly, as Betty sobbed on her shoulder.

John came up at this moment, and they both tried to push the heavy logs away, but could not move them an inch, even with all their strength. At one time it really seemed as if Betty must remain there all night.

"It's no use pulling any more," panted Madge, scarlet from her efforts. "I shall run up to Papa's workshop and get his little axe. Then I can chop away the log enough for her to get out."

Possibly Betty was terrified by the prospect of having an axe wielded by alarmingly energetic but unskilled hands too near her foot. At all events she not only dried her tears at this suggestion, but twisted her ankle so actively about that it slipped out of the crack as mysteriously as it had gone in. There was no harm done, except various bruises which had been chiefly caused by her efforts to escape.

In spite of some natural disappointment at not having any occasion to exhibit her powers as a woodcutter, Madge congratulated her sister heartily on getting loose, and the three children returned towards the house. Miss Thompson was looking for them in the garden. They ran up to her, concluding that as usual they were late for tea and she had come to remind them of it.

"For once you are wrong," she said. "At least it is just tea-time, but that was not why I was trying to find you. Now wash your hands, brush your hair, and go to the schoolroom. There you will find three visitors."

CHAPTER XXII
THE VISITORS

The children were far quicker than usual in carrying out Miss Thompson's directions and preparing themselves for tea. They were exceedingly curious to see the visitors, who, contrary to all custom, seemed to have been shown into the school-room instead of the drawing-room. And yet they were also a little shy, so that there was none of the usual crowding at the doorway in trying who should enter first. The younger ones very contentedly stood aside and allowed Madge to take the lead without a murmur.

An elderly person, in a large black velvet bonnet, sat with her back to the window, a very gaily-dressed little girl standing by her side. The children looked vacantly from one to the other, wondering why they had come.

"Well, Madge!" exclaimed Miss Thompson, "how much longer are you going to stand there before you speak to Mrs. Winter, who has come all the way from Churchbury to bring you a present?"

"Of course it's Mrs. Winter!" cried Madge, who had really been completely mystified by the presence of the best black velvet bonnet, so unlike the rather shabby straw hat in which Mrs. Winter had helped to search for the missing brown bag.

"And this is Mrs. Winter's grandchild," continued Miss Thompson. "Her name is Ann—"

"Is that Ann?" cried three excited voices; and the children pressed eagerly forward to have a good look at the little girl who, though scarcely older than themselves, was frequently left in charge of a real shop.

Ann was a large solid-looking girl of thirteen, in a red cashmere frock that was hardly as bright as her plump cheeks. Her hair had evidently been plaited very tightly overnight, so that it stood out in a frizzled mass all round her head. The whole effect was very large and bright.

"I have brought you a new pet," said Mrs. Winter addressing Madge; "something you have seen before, but it looks rather different now." She opened a large basket that was on the floor beside her, and lifted out a pretty tortoise-shell cat.

"What a love!" cried Madge. "Is it the kitten we found in the cellar? But it looks quite big and fat now, only the colour is the same."

"Ah, it's wonderful what care and good feeding will do for any animal!" observed Mrs. Winter. "You remember how scared the poor creature was at first? Well, now she is so tame that she will sit on my shoulder. Just see."

While the cat exhibited two or three little tricks, such as standing on her hind legs to eat a bit of bread, Mrs. Winter explained that she had always intended to make a present of the pretty creature to the young lady who had been so frightened by her in the cellar.

"So, this being early-closing day in the town, I borrowed Mrs. Smith's pony-trap and drove out, bringing little Ann with me for company," she said.

"And Mrs. West wishes you to rest and have some tea before you return," added Miss Thompson. "So let us all sit down at once, and Pussy shall have a saucer to herself in the corner of the room."

When tea was finished the children asked permission to show Ann their gardens, and pick her a bunch of flowers before she returned to the town. Mrs. Winter preferred sitting indoors in the shade, until her grandchild was ready to start.

It must be owned that as long as they were in the schoolroom Ann had proved disappointingly dull. Instead of enlightening them on her method of keeping shop when she was left in sole charge, she sat stolidly munching cake, and hardly replying when she was spoken to by Miss Thompson. In point of fact poor Ann was rendered desperately shy by being dressed up in all her finest clothes to come on this important visit. All the way to Beechgrove her grandmother had been warning her that she must behave beautifully if they were asked to go inside the house, and the consequence was that the poor girl was almost afraid to speak, for fear of saying or doing the wrong thing. But when once in the garden her shyness of the young ladies rapidly faded away.

"Do you ever climb trees or sail boats in ditches?" inquired Madge, when they had at last got on easy conversational terms with their visitor.

Ann explained that there were only a limited number of trees in Churchbury, and that the police forbid any interference with them. "Of course some of the children sail their boats in the gutters after a storm," she added; "but Mother wouldn't like us to do that. She always makes us keep ourselves to ourselves."

"But here it's quite different!" broke in Madge. "We do just what we like, only there is rather a fuss if we tear our clothes very badly. You might begin on an easy tree."

"Perhaps she would like to see the pigs and cows first?" interposed Betty, who could not help noticing that their guest showed some natural reluctance to risk the red cashmere frock among unknown and probably prickly branches.

Ann had been afraid to say that she did not at all wish to climb trees, but she eagerly grasped at this chance of a reprieve, and they all set off towards the pig-sty. Now the young Wests always regarded the little farmyard over which Barton presided as far the most interesting part of Beechgrove. If their mother had visitors she invariably took them to see the greenhouses, a dull sort of entertainment, as it seemed to the children. Certainly some people would stand for half an hour in front of a row of pots asking questions and reading the names on wooden labels. It seemed incredible that they should derive amusement from this monotonous performance, so the children concluded that they did it merely because some such absurd custom was demanded by good manners of all guests. Now, looking at the pigs was quite a different affair. There was some pleasure to be got out of that, and as Ann stood on tiptoe to peep over the wooden door of the sty they felt convinced that they were giving her an unusual treat.

Unfortunately, one has to be accustomed to pigs to appreciate them properly. When a gigantic old sow was at last lured out of her sleeping apartment by a shower of acorns, artfully thrown against her flabby sides, the Wests shrieked with delight because she was followed by her whole family.

"I never saw them all out before although they are nearly a month old," observed Madge, wishing delicately to impress upon the stranger that she was unusually lucky.

"We never saw them all out before," echoed John. "You see there are three in the trough, and one all sticky who has just crawled out, that makes four. Then there are five squeezed up in the mud behind the sow's back and two under her snout, so you can see the whole eleven at once. She had thirteen, but two of them were squashed to death the first day. Barton found them both flat; he says she must have slept on top of them by mistake. Our sows generally do when they have a lot of children."

"Do you notice that little black one with a white patch under his right eye?" inquired Betty, feeling that it was now her turn to do the honours of the pig-sty. "We call him Spot. He is such a little love, only horribly greedy. That is why he is in such a mess, he will crawl in the trough and get covered with milk. Sometimes Barton brings him outside for us to pat. I wonder if we could possibly get him for ourselves if we poked the sow off with sticks so that she shouldn't push through the door when it is opened?"

"Oh, don't try! Please don't open the door!" begged Ann. "I couldn't bear to have those horrid smelly creatures coming after me. I know I should scream if they got loose!"

"Don't you like pigs, then?" This inquiry came in tones of astonishment from all three children.

"Like them? No! They smell that horrid it quite upsets me!" Poor Ann's disgust was so genuine that she quite forgot to speak as correctly as she had succeeded in doing up to this point.

It was in vain that the Wests pointed out how baby pigs are quite as pretty as kittens or puppies when they roll playfully over on their mother's fat sides. Ann only held her nose and turned away her face; even when Spot went through the most ridiculous antics, pulling his little brother Whitey all about the sty by his tail, she expressed no admiration.

"Well, if you really don't like them I suppose we had better go and see the cows," said Madge rather impatiently. It is always disappointing, and gives very unnecessary trouble, when visitors will not share one's own tastes. Madge had relied on the pigs as an enormous attraction to a town child, and she was proportionately irritated when the entertainment failed. "I suppose you don't think cows dirty?" she asked with elaborate politeness.

No, Ann had no objection to cows. On the contrary, she knew a milkman who kept some cows on the outskirts of the town, and she sometimes went there and had a tumbler of new milk for a treat. To be sure she felt a little timid when Madge pushed a cabbage into her hand, and told her to feed a large red cow with particularly sharp horns. The children had a habit of each adopting a cow and feeding it themselves when there were any cabbages or pea-stalks to spare. Every cow, of course, had a name.

"That red one is quite new. She only came on Saturday," observed John. "So we haven't yet settled who she is to belong to, and that is why you can feed her. But we are going to call her Spiteful, because she shakes her head so crossly and has such very sharp horns."

This was rather a formidable introduction to a cow, and it is not to be wondered at that Ann soon incurred the scorn of the other children by dropping her cabbage on the ground and retiring behind the railings. She afterwards accused Spiteful of having tried to bite her.

"Well, if you don't care for feeding the animals perhaps you would like to play in the hay-loft?" said Madge with calm patience.

"Oh, yes! That is just what I should like!" cried Ann eagerly. A loft seemed to present fewer possibilities of danger than any of the other places of amusement to which they had yet taken her.

There was a little difficulty about climbing a ladder out of the yard. Ann was awkward, and the red cashmere dress being rather long she continually tripped over it. But when they had once safely reached the loft they had a grand game of play among the great heaps of hay and straw, scattering them untidily all over the neatly-swept floor in a way that was certain to drive Barton almost wild whenever he discovered it.

The distant ringing of a large bell at last broke in upon the children's shouts.

"That is to call us," explained Madge. "They always ring it when we are out in the fields and forget tea. But it can't be tea now because we have had it. I expect Mrs. Winter wants to go home."

"Oh, whatever will Grandmama say when she sees my dress!" wailed Ann as they emerged from the gloom of the loft into full daylight. "It was new to go to London," she continued sadly; "and Mother said it would do to wear on Sundays all through the year."

The red cashmere had indeed suffered sadly. It bore greasy traces of having been in contact with the pig-sty door all down its front, and was also torn in more than one place. Mrs. Winter was very much distressed by her grandchild's appearance when they returned to the house, and scolded her somewhat severely for having behaved in a rough and unmannerly fashion when out on a visit. Poor Ann burst into tears, and was only partially comforted when Miss Thompson took her upstairs and kindly stitched together the worst of the rents so that she might not look absolutely ragged on her way home.

When the little pony cart drove away from the door Madge returned rather thoughtfully to the schoolroom with the tortoise-shell cat in her arms.

"It seems a curious thing," she said, "that people are not always happy when you mean them to be. I thought Ann would like the same things as we do, and after all she has gone away almost crying, and hasn't enjoyed herself a bit."

"Another time," answered Miss Thompson, "when you really wish to give your guests pleasure, you had better consult their tastes instead of your own. If you had only considered for a moment, it was not probable that a town child would be as familiar with animals as you are; and it was also easy to see that Ann had been dressed in her best clothes for the afternoon and was afraid of hurting them."

"Perhaps so," said Madge. "But I always think it's rather stupid of people who don't like the same things as we do, don't you?"

CHAPTER XXIII
AN END OF HIDING

At the earliest opportunity on the following day Madge, Betty, and John returned to the loft to finish their interrupted game. They were three cavaliers hiding from Cromwell's soldiers, and really a better place of concealment could not have been found than the loft, where by simply closing a door they were in almost complete darkness. Madge, as captain, neglected no opportunity of ensuring the safety of her followers. She made them crouch down behind the straw, and lie so still that even the most sharp-sighted Roundheads would scarcely have suspected their existence.

"I will steal out to keep watch," she whispered, creeping on her hands and knees towards the closed door. "Posted by the crack of the hinges I can survey the whole country, and watch the march of the rebel troops without being seen. Then when— Oh!"

The door suddenly flew open in her face, almost knocking her over. A head appeared at the top of the ladder. It was Lewis Brand's!

If the children had really been discovered by Cromwell's soldiers they could hardly have been more frightened. Lewis had time to step off the ladder and come into the loft before they recovered themselves sufficiently to speak.

"You don't seem overjoyed to see a friend?" he remarked sneeringly.

"Oh, do go away!" cried Betty nervously. "Somebody will see you! I know they will!"

"It's very kind of you to be so anxious on my account, but I think I can take care of myself," said Lewis with a disagreeable laugh. "You thought you had all got away from me, did you? Pretty sort of friends, I call you! All going off one day without saying a word, and never coming back."

"After all, we are not obliged to play with you!" exclaimed Madge with some spirit.

"Aren't you indeed? We shall soon see!" replied Lewis. "I'm not at all sure that you can get away from me! I sat on the wall and watched you come down here after dinner, then I seized my opportunity when nobody was about, and ran across the fields to join you. It was worth seeing how frightened you all were when I quietly stepped in at the door! And wherever you go to play I shall turn up in just the same way. You see if I don't!"

"What nonsense! We can play in the garden if we like!" said Madge defiantly.

"So you can! And find me hiding in the potting-shed and behind the cucumber-frames," replied Lewis.

Betty began to cry. It was not very brave of her, but then she had been rejoicing so much at getting rid of Lewis and his mysteries, and was so horribly disappointed when they all returned.

"I won't have you coming back here to tease us all!" cried Madge angrily. "I am sorry we ever spoke to you. It was wrong of us, and I heartily wish we hadn't. If you go on—"

"Mind, you promised faithfully not to tell anybody about me," interrupted Lewis. "If you say a single word about my coming over the wall you will have told a lie."

"Yes, that's the worst of it," admitted Madge. "And yet it seems just as untruthful to meet you and pretend we are only playing by ourselves. Either way it's wrong."

"Very likely," said Lewis carelessly. "That's your affair. It's too late to draw back now."

There was a silence, during which the three Wests heartily repented their naughty folly in having secretly made such an undesirable acquaintance.

Presently there was a heavy footstep in the yard below.

"What's that?" whispered Lewis, in a very different voice to the bullying accents in which he had just been speaking.

"It is Barton driving the cows into the yard to be milked," replied Madge softly. "He always does it about this time."

"But how am I to get down the ladder to go home if he is standing at the bottom?" inquired Lewis nervously.

"I never thought of that! He will be in the yard for the next hour," answered Madge. "Of course we don't mind passing him, because we are allowed to play up here; only he doesn't like us making the hay as untidy as it is now. But I'm sure you can't get down without being seen."

"You won't all run away and leave me caught like a rat in a trap, will you?" begged Lewis, almost whimpering with fright.

"Is it likely?" replied Madge in her finest tone of scorn. "Stay quiet," she added with contemptuous kindness, "and we will get you out of it somehow."

It is in moments of peril that a true leader shines most. While Lewis lay cowering behind the straw, and the twins waited expectantly for some suggestion, Madge calmly looked round the loft and originated a plan. "I know how you can get away," she said, after some moments of earnest thought. "There is that little door at the back of the loft, it does not look out into the yard but out upon the hay-ricks, in fact that is where they put the hay up into the loft. If you get down that side Barton can't possibly see you while he is milking the cows in the yard."

"Oh, that's a capital idea! I'll go at once!" cried Lewis. "Not that I am really afraid of your old man or anybody," he added, with a return of his customary boastful manner. "Only I don't want to get you all into trouble."

"You have become very brave all of a sudden," said Madge, who by this time heartily despised him for his mixture of bragging and cowardice. "It's fortunate you are not afraid of anything," she added rather maliciously, "because you see there is no ladder outside this door, so you will have to drop down to the ground as best you can."

"It isn't very far, I suppose?" asked Lewis anxiously. But when the loft door was at last opened—rather a difficult job to accomplish quietly, as the hinges were rusty and would creak,—he declared that he could not possibly get down without a ladder.

"But you must!" exclaimed Madge impatiently. "It's your only chance of getting away without being seen."

"I shall be hurt! I know I shall!" moaned Lewis, as he drew back with a shiver from the open door.

"It isn't so very far," said Betty encouragingly. "Not higher than a room, I think."

Still Lewis hung back. "Oh, dear Madge," he whined, "couldn't you manage to carry the ladder round from the yard to the door at the back?"

"Well, if you can't possibly get down without it I will try!" said Madge desperately. "Betty and John must come with me, as the ladder is so long I can't carry it alone. I am afraid Barton will make a fuss when he sees us moving it, though."

"Oh no, he won't! I dare say he won't notice you," asserted Lewis, only intent on his own safety, and not caring in the least what risks other people ran on his account.

But in the excitement of the moment the children had raised their voices rather loudly, and Barton heard them as he milked the cows in the yard below.

"Now, you young ladies and Master John, you are breaking that straw all to pieces, I'll be bound!" he shouted. "I'll be up and see what you are about directly I've done with this cow, that I will! Tossing the hay all over the floor, when it was only put tidy the other day!"

"Will he come up really?" whispered Lewis, white with terror. "Yes? Oh, help me to get away! Help me!"

"I will try," said Madge, once more taking the lead; "but you must do as I tell you. Now if you had a rope to hold on to do you think you could get down to the ground?"

"Yes, I think I could. But where is the rope? Please be quick!"

"Of course we can't get a rope here!" answered Madge sharply. She was losing all patience with this coward, who only thought of his own comfort and safety. However, she had pledged herself to do her best for him, so she continued: "We will tie all our pocket-handkerchiefs together. They will reach a good way towards the ground."

This really seemed an excellent idea, although when it came to be worked out John could not make any contribution, having left his handkerchief in the pocket of another coat. The knots also took up a terrible amount of material, so that the completed rope was not a very long affair.

"Do you think it is strong?" asked Lewis nervously. "And that you can hold my weight?"

"No fear of that!" Madge squatted down by the door, Betty held her firmly by the waist, and John tugged at the back. "Now we are ready," they said.

There was really no excuse for any further delay. Lewis desperately seized the end of the knotted handkerchiefs and stood for a moment irresolute on the edge of the wall. Then suddenly, thinking he heard Barton coming behind him, he sprang forward with such a jerk that the handkerchiefs slipped through his fingers and he fell heavily to the ground.

"Well, that is his own fault, not ours!" exclaimed Madge. "We held the rope tight enough, and if he chose to jump in that silly way nobody could help it!" Her indignation, however, gave way to fear, as Lewis continued to lie motionless on the ground. "Is he hurt, or only shamming?" she said. "Lewis! Lewis! get up and run home before anyone sees you!" Even this appeal produced no effect on the prostrate figure, and the children became seriously alarmed.

"I don't think he can be pretending," observed Betty; "he would be afraid to lie there so near the yard. Besides, he is in such a funny position."

"I must go down and see what is the matter," said Madge decidedly. "No, I sha'n't try the handkerchiefs, we have had enough of them, and I don't think you two really are strong enough to hold me up." Without waiting to discuss the matter any further she climbed down the ladder and ran through the yard.

"Hullo, Miss Madge, where are you off to?" cried old Barton from the corner of the cow-house. "Up to some mischief again, I can see by the pace you are running? Whatever have you been doing now, I wonder?"

Madge rushed on without answering, and disappeared round the end of the buildings. Lewis was still lying in a sort of crumpled-up heap when she reached him. He did not attempt to rise or even speak when she pulled him by the arm. "I am afraid he must be badly hurt!" she cried anxiously to Betty and John, who were staring with white frightened faces from the open door of the loft above.

LEWIS WAS STILL LYING IN A SORT OF CRUMPLED-UP HEAP

"What shall you do?" they asked. "Will he get better? Can we help?"

"It's something too bad for us. I shall call Barton to look at him," replied Madge. There were exclamations of astonishment from the twins. "Yes, it's no good trying to keep it a secret about Lewis any longer," she said gravely. "Of course we shall be scolded, but that can't be helped."

When Barton came he took a very grave view of the case. "Seems as if the young gentleman were mortal bad," he said. "Better run up to the house and call someone at once. It's a question if he ever walks home again, wherever he comes from!"

"Does Barton mean he will die?" asked John in an awestruck whisper as the three children ran off for help. Nobody cared to be left behind with Barton by the side of that still figure on the ground.

"Oh no! Barton only said that to try and frighten us," answered Madge with a would-be hopeful air. But in her heart fear that Lewis was already dead so overcame all other considerations that she rushed into the house calling for help without a moment's thought of the blame she was about to incur.

Fortunately Captain West was at home that afternoon. He understood at once that somebody was hurt while doing something in the loft, and naturally concluded that it was old Barton, whose business it was to carry down the hay when wanted.

"Did he slip on the ladder?" inquired Captain West as he hurried back with the children.

"Oh no! getting out of that little square door at the back of the loft. You see, he was sliding down our handkerchiefs and they slipped—"

"Barton sliding down your handkerchiefs?" repeated Captain West in a tone of great astonishment.

"No, of course not!" laughed Madge rather hysterically. "It was Lewis— that's to say, a boy who came over the wall—when we were in the Eagle's Nest, you know."

"I don't know in the least what you are talking about," said Captain West; "but I can see he is badly hurt," he added as they came in sight of Lewis lying just as he fell, for old Barton had been afraid of trying to move him alone.

"Look here," began Captain West after a short examination of the injured boy, "you, Betty, run back to the house and ask your mother to send for the doctor. Don't frighten her more than you can help. John, go and fetch the gardener as quickly as possible; we must get this poor boy carried home and properly attended to. Now, Madge," he added when the twins had started on their errands, "collect yourself, please, and speak the truth. Where does this boy come from?"

"From Mrs. Howard's, over the wall," answered Madge quietly, though she could not help trembling with excitement. "He lives with her and is very cruelly treated, so we began to talk one day when we were in the Eagle's Nest, and—"

"That will do for the present," interrupted Captain West. "Now I don't want any of you here any more. Go off to the schoolroom and stay there till bed-time, unless I send for you."

CHAPTER XXIV
EXPLANATIONS

After so much excitement it seemed intolerably dull to sit quietly hour after hour in the schoolroom without knowing what was going on. Even Miss Thompson could not attend to them, for she was sitting with their mother, who happened to be unwell in bed. The children had time to talk over and imagine every kind of terrible conclusion to the accident before their father was ready to come and see them.

"Will he get better?" Madge inquired in a trembling voice as soon as the door opened.

"Get better? Yes, I should hope so in every way," answered Captain West, sitting down and taking the twins gently on his knees, while Madge hung over the back of his chair. "It's a bad accident though," he continued. "A broken leg and some injury to the head. He only regained consciousness just before I left Mrs. Howard's."

"Oh, what were they doing with him? I hope they won't lock him into the cellar now he is ill!" cried Betty compassionately.

"My dear child! What are you thinking about? Do we usually lock people in cellars when they are ill?" laughed her father. "No, he was in a remarkably nice bedroom, with a hospital nurse and Dr. Brown in attendance on him when I left."

Betty felt greatly relieved. It seemed impossible to believe that much cruelty would take place in the presence of Dr. Brown, who always ordered her black-currant tea when she had a cough, and told Nurse to put as little mustard as possible in the poultices.

"But why should you expect that boy to be ill-treated at home?" inquired Captain West. "From what I hear about him I should think it is much more likely he has been spoilt!"

"Ah! it isn't his real home," explained Betty, "and that Mrs. Howard is a terrible person."

She was going to add that the old lady had the reputation of being a witch, but the accusation seemed too absurd to be urged in broad daylight in the school-room. So she only mentioned a few of Lewis's tales about Mrs. Howard's cruelty to him.

Captain West listened for a minute and then fairly burst out laughing. "Do you really mean that you believed all that?" he said. "You seriously thought boys were stolen, and shut up in dark cellars, and all the rest of it?"

The children hung their heads, suddenly feeling rather ashamed of the ease with which they had been imposed upon, for they could see that their father did not believe a word of the horrors.

"But other people beside Lewis Brand have told us that Mrs. Howard is very dreadful and mysterious," observed Madge, who did not at all like finding herself quite in the wrong. "When Mrs. Bunn is weeding the garden she sometimes tells us what people in the village say—"

"She would be better employed pulling up groundsel!" interrupted Captain West. "But what does she tell you about starving boys in cellars full of black-beetles?"

Madge was bound to admit that she had never heard this particular accusation against Mrs. Howard from anybody except Lewis.

"But people say she is mad and never will see strangers. And we have looked at her over the wall, so we know something about it," she persisted.

"And you saw a very delicate-looking old lady tottering along and nodding her head? Just so. Now listen to me. Many years ago poor Mrs. Howard had a very serious illness, which left her with some disease of the nerves so that she cannot keep her head still for a moment. Ever since then she has shut herself up and avoided seeing strangers, as she is very shy about her infirmity being noticed. And I must say," concluded Captain West, "that I am vexed to think my children should have tried to pry into what did not in the least concern them."

"I am sorry we looked at her, if that is the reason she nodded so funnily to the cows," said Madge. "But were not any of the stories Lewis told us true? About the cellars, and the jailer with the gray beard?"

"I cannot tell you anything definite about Mrs. Howard's cellars, except that, judging by the size of the house, they must be very small," answered Captain West. "But this I know for a fact. The boy Lewis Brand is an orphan with no money of his own, and Mrs. Howard being an old friend of his parents generously offered to adopt him and bring him up. Unfortunately, owing to his mother's long illness, Lewis was very much neglected as a child, and got into such bad habits that he has been nothing but an anxiety to his kind friend from the first. He has already been expelled from two schools, and Mrs. Howard is at present trying to educate him at home with a tutor—that gentleman with the gray beard you saw."

"Well, I never heard of such a horrid story-telling boy!" exclaimed Madge impetuously. "And so ungrateful too! But why should he have told such dreadful untruths about Mrs. Howard?"

"To frighten you, I expect," replied Captain West. "The reason they would not keep him at school was because he would tease and frighten the younger boys. He seems a born bully."

"And a great coward into the bargain!" added Madge. "You should have seen how frightened—"

"I dare say!" interrupted her father. "The two things generally go together. His only excuse is that he was badly trained when young. However, you will probably admit that in future it will be wiser to let us choose your friends for you?"

The children had no answer to make. They were thoroughly ashamed of themselves. When their father left the room they began to discuss the subject in all its bearings.

"I don't want to abuse Lewis as he is ill," said Madge. "That would be mean. But I must tell you both something very suspicious that happened. When I was standing by him just after he fell from the loft I happened to step on something hard. I stooped to see what it was, picked it up, and here it is!"

"One of my marbles!" cried John. "One of those I lost out of the treasure-house! I am quite sure it is, because of the funny red mark I painted myself on the side."

"You did it with my new paints," chimed in Betty.

"But how did the marble come there?" asked John, much bewildered, but holding tightly on to his newly-recovered treasure for fear it should again disappear.

"Well, of course I can't tell for certain," said Madge. "I can only guess. But it seems as if it must have fallen out of Lewis's pocket."

"Then you think he took our things out of the treasure-hole?" cried Betty. "He never could have been so wicked as to steal them, and then come pretending he was so sorry for our loss and wondering where they had gone!"

"Perhaps he didn't actually mean to steal them, only to tease us," suggested Madge. "And I feel sure now that he took the rope-ladder," she continued. "You know he pretended at the time that he couldn't get up the wall without it; but that was only to deceive us. He had those iron railings for ladders, though he said nothing about them until later."

"Oh, Madge!" exclaimed the twins. They could think of nothing else to say. The contemplation of such deliberate perfidy was too overpowering. The more they recalled Lewis's dark hints and malicious suggestions about other people, the more disgusted they felt with him, and the more vexed with themselves for having been so completely deceived. "We might have known there was something wrong when he made us promise not to say anything about him!" they said. "Never again will we have a secret friend!"

Captain West went several times to see Lewis during his long illness, and did his best to make the unfortunate boy understand the reason why he was an unfit companion for other children. At first Lewis seemed to regard his untruths and deceptions merely in the light of very clever jokes; but gradually some faint sense of shame appeared to steal over him, though whether on account of his faults or only because they had been discovered, Captain West could not very well make out.

"What will become of Lewis Brand?" asked the children one day when their father had just returned from visiting him.

"Directly he is well enough to walk he is going to live with a gentleman who has great experience with boys, and who will do his best to counteract the faults that you all find so shameful in Lewis," said Captain West. "But in justice to the poor boy I must add one thing. He was much neglected as a little child, and had none of the advantages of an affectionate and careful training. Now, in proportion to his opportunities, perhaps he did not behave worse than certain children who, with no excuses at all, tried to deceive—"

"Do you mean us?" interrupted Madge, with a very red face. She did not at all appreciate being compared in any way with Lewis, for whose conduct she felt great contempt. And yet there was a certain element of truth in her father's words that could not be ignored.

"Well, we will say no more about that," continued Captain West cheerfully. "I think after what has happened I can trust you all not to embark again on secret friendships with strangers?"

"No! Indeed we will not!" cried the three children. And they kept their resolution.